She Settled It Within

Carolyn Wells

Published by Carolyn Wells, 2023.

This is a work of fiction. Similarities to real people, places, or events are entirely coincidental.

SHE SETTLED IT WITHIN

First edition. July 3, 2023.

Copyright © 2023 Carolyn Wells.

ISBN: 978-1005868550

Written by Carolyn Wells.

Table of Contents

She Settle It Within

Copyright 2023 Madam CJ. Wells
Published by Madam CJ. Wells at Smashwords

BUTTERFLY ONE: STARTING OVER

It was May of 1989 and a new day had dawned for Karen. The sky was a beautiful blue, and the sun shone at a perfect temperature in the city. Karen had just moved into her new apartment with her daughter, Kenyuna. The excitement was almost too much for her to contain. Karen knew what lay ahead for her in the new town, and the anticipation raged inside her chest. But she did not imagine that in her life she would share the statistics of so many other single, divorced, and head-of-household women. Taking a deep breath, she settled into her new apartment with just the bare necessities to get her started. As she looked around, she found some bathroom items, kitchen utensils, and a covering for the bed that was in storage boxes—boxes with all the clothes she and Kenyuna owned that came with them. She was glad she had shipped most of the boxes to her brother's house weeks before the final decision was made to leave her abusive husband.

The items would have to be enough to get her started with the new life for now. She had suffered a great loss with the discussion of leaving a marriage and a man she had once loved so dearly. With no doubts in her mind, she knew it was the right thing to do for herself as well as for Kenyuna. The choice had been made, and there was no turning back now; they would have to make do with these few items. The household items came in handy with preparing morning and evening meals for Kenyuna and herself. Karen knew it would be hard times for her for a while, especially with very little money. She had to sell some items to get the money she needed to leave her husband. It was only enough to put a first and last month's payment on an apartment, with a few thousand dollars to keep her off from work for a few months at most if she was extremely frugal with her spending.

Deep within, Karen knew she would do whatever it took to make life better for herself and Kenyuna. She reminded herself that she was up for the challenge and had come too far to have doubts about her decisions. Karen arranged the few items she had around the small apartment to give it a more at-home atmosphere and welcome feel, but the other rooms would be bare for now. Karen never had to stand on her own before, but there was no one else to help her make decisions in the best interest of herself and Kenyuna.

She felt a nervous tick in her stomach that made her feel afraid for a moment. Her attention moved toward tonight when they would start sleeping on the floor until things got better. She did not complain.

One night would turn into many nights on that floor as it became the resting place that gave her and Kenyuna the night's rest they would need for the days ahead. Karen and Kenyuna would often say their prayers and give thanks for a safe place to lay their heads. A safe place on the floor without the comforts of a bed felt good. Even if it was not real, it felt safe. Each full day was a good day, regardless of the shortage of money. Karen applied for several job positions during the day while Kenyuna was in school. She left early for the library to submit applications online and pick up newspapers in the city with job postings. She needed to find a job quickly because time was of the essence.

She noticed a position with a company called Pay-less Cash-ways Freight Company on the paper and applied, not expecting to get a call. She didn't have any experience, and she had never worked in freight before. She did not have any plans to go out today, as she would spend the day going over her options just in case no jobs came through. The phone rang, and the caller asked for her. The caller wanted to know if she could come in for an interview for a part-time position as a clerk. Karen didn't even ask what the hours were or how much the salary was. She thanked God, knowing that the extra money would be a great help right about now.

She worked five days a week from 10:00 am. to 3:00 pm., which worked out great. The money was enough to pay the monthly rent with a little extra to finally send for her other items in storage. The new job had Karen thinking about moving closer to the office because the bus ride was not always pleasant. If she moved closer to the city, she could walk to work each day and catch the bus during the cold weather.

Karen learned a lot about the freight industry, including how different materials are shipped and how rates change depending on the material and where in the country it is being shipped to. Karen thought this would be great for her to ship her items, and she smiled at how things were working out. She checked the costs of several freighting companies she dealt with and requested price quotes. Karen knew that freight companies billed by the pound, and she thought she only had about two hundred pounds or less in storage. The cost would be very little, if not free, with her employee discount. She contacted the company with the lower quoted price and delivery service fees; the winner was the Roadway Company.

She would be especially happy to see Kenyuna's old canopy bed, which she purchased some years ago and should look pretty new like the last time she saw it. She could see the white and gold trim on the headboard; she would be glad to see it and was even happier that she decided not to sell it. Karen called her friend a few weeks before with details and information about the pick-up time. Angela promised to keep Karen's storage items and pay for them each month until Karen was settled, and she promised to send them to her when she needed them. She was surprised at how quickly time had passed once she realized it had been about six months, although it seemed like forever since she had slept in a bed. Karen didn't know how much longer she could sleep on that floor or even how much longer her body could stand it. The floor was tolerable for sleeping, but it was nothing like sleeping in a real bed. It was taking its toll on her, and she could feel it. She was not as young as she used to be, but she was not too old to start a new life for herself. Tonight, she would sleep in a real bed, with all the comfort that a bed could offer. Goodbye, sleeping on the floor.

She rose early the next morning and got Kenyuna ready for school. They waited for the school bus as she watched Kenyuna talking with the other children from the neighborhood. As soon as Kenyuna stepped on the bus and waved goodbye, Karen walked up the stairs to her apartment. She took a shower and dressed, hoping that the delivery truck would come early. Maybe she could get a few hours in at work today. Karen waited and waited, then decided she would rearrange items to make room for the additional furniture.

She thought about how Kenyuna wanted to stay home with her today. Karen knew Kenyuna was as excited about the furniture coming today as she was. Kenyuna had missed many of her favorite toys, especially the bike she had almost grown too big for. She had talked about that bike most of the evening until Karen told her it was time for bed and that her bike would be waiting for her when she got back from school the next day. Karen almost gave into her own excitement and let her stay home from school, but remembered that she had to learn how to stand her ground with her. Regardless of how much she loved Kenyuna, no was no, and yes was yes. That is what she would stick to, even in difficult times. She did not have to explain herself as a mom. This would be rule number one in her new life as a single parent. Karen knew she would not have time to watch Kenyuna and make sure she had received all her items.

She looked around for her checklist of stored items to compare with the driver's list. She needed to stay focused to check for different or lost items if any. She was glad she had sent Kenyuna to school after all; with her out of the way, even though it was just 9:00 am., it seemed like the day was longer. Karen looked at the clock, patiently waiting for the delivery truck. She looked out the window and listened in vain for the doorbell to sound. She wrote in her weekly planner and thought about what a long day she would have as she filled in the next few weeks. Between unpacking and Kenyuna, she might as well get ready for a long week ahead.

Karen's patience was wearing thin; she checked her watch. It was now 11:45 am. She took her mind off getting a few hours of work in today. That wasn't going to work out. She called her boss to let him know that she would not be in for work today. She had told him earlier that she should be there by 1:00 pm. for a few hours. She headed to organize items to make room for her other items. She paced back and forth for another fifteen minutes, which seemed like another hour had passed. She looked out the windows, again opening the balcony doors, and watched the highway in the distance. There was no truck for miles in her direction.

She thought about taking a nap; maybe that would take her mind off of all the things she had to do and did not want to do, but it was too late to take a nap. She stepped back inside, taking one long, hard look toward the road, and checked her watch again. The nap was out, and she did not make any money today; this would be a day she would remember.

Through the balcony doors, she saw a truck coming in her direction; surely it would keep going past like others this morning, but she stood for a moment watching it.

The truck turned toward the corner onto her street and came to a stop in front of her apartment as she looked on from the balcony. Karen composed herself and watched as she cleared her throat and waited to hear the doorbell ring. She was not sure if the driver saw her or not. She checked herself and started downstairs toward the door to greet the deliveryman as he rang the doorbell. Karen could see the deliveryman standing at the door, looking down at the papers in his hand. Karen opened the door. He stood silent for a brief moment as the seconds seemed like minutes.

Karen thought, "My goodness, what a good-looking black man." She composed herself as much as she could to ask, "May I help you?"

He stepped toward the door. Karen hoped she hadn't said what she was thinking out loud. He had an easy feeling about him, so she did not feel threatened as she stepped outside to greet him.

Loneliness has a way of creeping up on you when you least expect it, she told herself, so stay focused on the task at hand.

She took the paper from his hand and looked over it. It seemed to have all the items on her list, so she took a deep breath.

As he returned to the truck, she followed him. He unlocked the truck's back door, jumped inside, and began to slide items to the edge. He jumped back down to the ground, pulled the boxes from the edge, and set them on the sidewalk. Karen tried to keep up, but she could not because he was working fast. She could not believe that she had that much stuff. Karen began picking up one or two small boxes at a time, heading toward the open door as quietly as she could. She wondered, between trips, how in the hell she would get the larger boxes, a mattress, and the box spring up the stairs all by herself. Looking back in disgust because she would have to do all this alone, she cursed her ex-husband from within. Suddenly, she heard footsteps approaching from behind her, and when she turned around, he was carrying the box spring up the stairs behind her.

"Where would you like this to go?"

"Just drop it in the middle of the floor," she said.

They both moved back toward the stairs for more of the boxes. She picked up the smaller boxes, and he carried the larger ones. Before she knew it, everything was inside, in the middle of the living room floor. Karen felt good. A partner would be nice to have to help out in a situation like this. She knew she needed a real man in her life, and he seemed to be a good example of what she wanted.

"Thank you, God," she said under her breath.

A brother and sister bonding, she thought to herself. Of course, she would have done the same thing for him if he were in the same situation.

Maybe there are still some good men in the world after all, Karen thought. Even if they were far and few in between and hard to find these days, this one was making a good impression on her—oh, what did she know? She had not dated anyone. It wasn't a priority right now, and he didn't have to help or do anything. He was just the delivery person. His job was to leave her shipment at the address and be on his way. She knew it was her responsibility, not his, to get the items into the apartment.

Karen could not remember having so many boxes, but they were here now. When all the boxes were inside, he asked her to sign off on the delivery slip and gave her the outstanding balance from the invoice.

"Twenty-seven dollars. I will need to complete the bill," he said. Karen went to find her purse as quietly as possible while he waited at the door. She wrote out a check for the balance and could not believe that was all she owed. She was aware that all freight companies have a final bill after delivery, but she was surprised to pay this amount. She really did get a big discount on her shipment. She felt a little uneasy, feeling he was looking at her from the corner of his eyes. It made her very nervous.

Oh, Lord, she thought, and she quietly handed him the check.

"Is it possible that I can get your phone number?" He said, "I would like to call you sometime."

"Sure."

Maybe this town would be alright after all, she thought. She handed him one of her cards with everything he needed to contact her. They made plans for the following Saturday. He said he would call to arrange a time. Karen told him she would have to bring her daughter along. He said that would be okay with him. Karen told him goodbye and thanked him for helping her as he headed out the door. Karen felt like the energizer bunny. She rearranged furniture and cleaned for the next few hours before Kenyuna came home. Karen set the bed up, unpacked the boxes, and then she sat in the middle of the living room floor.

Why did everything end up in the middle of the living room instead of in the rooms it belonged in? She thought, but she didn't mind this time. She noticed the time on her watch. Before she knew it, Kenyuna's bus was outside, and she headed downstairs to greet her little girl. How excited Kenyuna would be to have her bike and some of her favorite toys! Karen was right. Kenyuna was happy to see her bike. It was the first thing she wanted to do: go right back outside and ride her bike. Karen did not disagree. She could use a break, and she was pretty excited too.

It was a good day, and Kenyuna deserved to have some fun with the other children in the neighborhood and show off her bike. They walked out the door as Karen set the bike down on the sidewalk. Kenyuna got on and off, and she went down the sidewalk with the biggest smile on her face. Karen was happy because her little girl was happy. The sun was going down, and the evening began to turn into darkness. Karen sat and watched Kenyuna ride up and down the sidewalk. She hoped this relationship she had with Kenyuna would last a lifetime. Would she do or say something wrong that would pull them apart as she grew older? Karen made the decision that she would be the mother and let Kenyuna be the child, and no matter what, that's the way it would be. In this new life, she would start out with new rules and regulations suitable for both of their new lives; they might as well start now. Karen could see that Kenyuna could stay outside forever riding her bike, but it was time to go inside, so Karen called for her.

It had been a long day for the both of them, and there was still much to do tomorrow. Kenyuna still had homework to do, dinner to prepare, a bath to take, and hair to do. Karen couldn't wait to lay her head on a bed. That would feel so good tonight. They said their prayers and climbed into bed under the covers, saying good night to each other. They were fast asleep.

***

Even before the alarm clock went off, Karen was awake, and even before Kenyuna woke up, she said a silent prayer to God. She thanked him for all the things he had brought and for making her little girl so happy yesterday. Karen knew in her heart that she had to make some major changes in her life. She wanted to do things differently in her new life. Karen headed toward the bathroom to shower. She smiled big at the progress she had made in such a short time. Things were moving into place. She could see the progress. She had really come a long way from where she had started. She had received her admission form to attend the community college during the fall. The part-time job was just enough to keep the household running with all the other assistance programs. It felt and looked like a home, and she had worked hard to make it safe for her and Kenyuna. She could relax a little from worrying about things, but they still needed to appreciate the things that they had.

She thought about applying for child support, but after she thought long and hard about the condition she left her ex-husband in over a year ago, she decided it would just be a waste of time. She was doing better without him and really did not want anything to do with him ever again; perhaps he would change over time. Karen would use whatever means necessary to achieve her goal and make damn sure that her little girl would suffer limited damage from the fallout of a deadbeat father. As far as she could tell, Kenyuna was doing pretty well, but she could not tell what the future would hold for her. Karen understood the importance of having both parents; she realized she could only be a mother, and fathers play a big part in a girl's life as well. As a mother, she would do her best to give her what she needed. Kenyuna needed and wanted a relationship with her father; she would have to deal with that later in the future. As for right now, Karen needed to stay focused on making sure they were both happy. Nothing else mattered to her. Karen resolved the issue of child support within herself; it would not be good for her. She really did not want any contact with him. Kenyuna would not get a penny for years; by then she would be an adult.

Her father may have been a good father for several years of her life, but now he was not the same father nor the man Karen had once loved. She often heard stories from family and friends that assured her that she had done the right thing when she divorced him and that she was the one who was better off. Another year later, Karen heard her ex-husband had two other children, and then he had three children, and then four other children. He had no job or place to live and was in and out of jail. Someone tried to kill him in the drug world. Karen felt sad, but she didn't want to tell her little girl that her father had died or been killed by someone. She was thankful that his lifestyle did not affect Kenyuna, and that was all that mattered to her. Karen would never tell her or even let on that the father she loved was a drug user. She let Kenyuna love him as she knew him to be. Karen knew that time would reveal all Kenyuna needed to know about her father. Karen would keep her as safe and secure as possible for as long as she could.

Winter was coming fast. Karen needed to get their winter clothes unpacked and ready for the cold days ahead. Her classes would begin in a few weeks, and she knew she needed all that done before then. She needed all the extra time to study for classes, help Kenyuna with homework, prepare meals, do assignments, and study for a test. She would have to keep a planner for this busy schedule, for sure.

Motherhood agreed with her, and she enjoyed her independence to make decisions that would either break her or make her a better person. She was pretty content with her life, although she had not had a date for months. She and Eugene still kept in contact, but she was just too busy with her life to be in a full-time relationship with him, and she felt the feeling was mutual. Whether they got together on the weekend or not, it did not bother her at all. She was either buried in her books, had a test to study for, or had a writing assignment due. Kenyuna was the only person who could break her studying time; anyone else was out of the question. She came to the conclusion in her mind that it would be better to just let the sleeping dog lie and stay focused on the task at hand while getting herself together. Karen did just that; she worked part-time while attending to Kenyuna's needs.

She studied hard to get through the classes with As, B's, and maybe a few Cs. She realized that college was not for the faint of mind or heart. It was hard work. She finished high school years ago and had only spent a few semesters in college before dropping out because she got pregnant with Kenyuna and got married. She geared her mind up and told herself that she could do this college experience with no sweat.

"Stay focused, stay focused," she told herself daily.

Karen was so focused that she did not see the change coming her way. It was the end of the first semester of classes, and to her surprise, she had completed it with a GPA of 3.0, feeling ready to take on the next level of college with confidence. However, things do not always turn out the way you expect them to. Just when you don't expect something to happen in life, prepare for it to happen. She had finally gotten her schedule working the way she wanted. Things were moving at a mostly stress-free pace. The weekdays worked like clockwork: home, school, Kenyuna, and rest for the next day. That was how her days went. It would be her schedule for a long while, and it worked just fine with her. Her instinct was reliable. She could count on it, and when things were going well, she felt just as good. Karen stayed on track with her studying as her courses began to get easier from semester to semester. She could not believe a year had passed with her GPA looking pretty good.

Financial assistance helped with her school supplies and some living expenses. She became an accountant without even taking a class to certify her profession. She juggled money like a real pro, keeping rent, utilities, and other expenses on track. She was feeling good about herself and what she had accomplished by turning a bad situation into a positive one. But the feeling of something being out of place kept her on edge. It had nothing to do with her ex-husband. He did not have a clue where she was, and she really did not know many people in this city.

What could give her this uneasy feeling? She could not put her finger on it, so she pushed the thought out of her mind. She was on a mission, and her deadline was approaching fast. She needed to complete it without any distractions. She didn't have time to focus on something she couldn't change, but she kept a watchful lookout. For months, nothing happened; the daily routine became the normal pattern from weeks to months.

Karen felt the opposite sex partner was null and void in her daily routine. Although she met plenty of eligible bachelors and suitors on the college campus, from the young to the old, she often blew them off. She was good at blowing them off because she had too much on her plate. She could not add another thing or person to it, even if she wanted to. She kept as close as possible to her schedule, promising herself she would not let anything interrupt the lifestyle she had started for herself and Kenyuna.

A new semester was approaching, and she would start hitting the books again in eight weeks. That was when she met Tasha. She sat across the room in the same class. Within the second week of the class, Tasha was having some trouble with the algebra class. Karen thought she would volunteer to help her, and at the same time, they would help each other to get a passing grade in this class. They studied before and after class, during lunch break, or just sat in the college courtyard on a warm day. Each week, the teacher would test or quiz the class over the last few weeks of class assignments. Karen knew she needed to be prepared for it; this teacher made sure you were going to learn algebra. Karen knew this class was going to be a challenge for her; it was a subject that was not one of her strong suits. She welcomed all the help she could get from her new classmate. Karen did not want to take this class over, so she hit the algebra book hard.

BUTTERFLY TWO: OUT OF THE BLUE THEN CAME YOU

Tasha could not stay after school. She had to go home and get her child off the school bus. It was early release day at their school, so she asked Karen if they could get together later to study at her house. Karen did not normally hang out at other people's homes. She was a little hesitant for a few moments but decided she would. She didn't want Tasha to feel that she did not trust her or think that she was weird or something. She told Tasha she would meet her at her house within a few hours just to let her check on something at home and make sure Kenyuna made it home from school safely.

Tasha's apartment was nice and neat, just not as clean as Karen's place. She did not feel too uncomfortable sitting at the kitchen table going over some algebra problems. While discussing several problems, Karen heard a door open, and in walked a handsome young man.

"Hi, Donnell," Tasha said.

"What's up?" he replied.

"Karen, this is my brother, Donnell," she said. "He lives with me until he gets his sh*t together."

He walked toward another room without a response. Karen could feel him looking in her direction, and it made her feel uneasy.

"Okay, Tasha," Karen said. "I've got to go."

"Thanks, girl. I will see you tomorrow."

Donnell came to the kitchen. "It was nice meeting you," he said.

"Nice meeting you, Donnell," Karen said as she walked out the door.

Home Sweet Home

Karen thought it had been a long day, and she was just ready to go to bed. She could hear the bed calling her, and she was listening, with sleep not far behind. Kenyuna was right behind her; she was now old enough to stay home for a few hours, but not many more. Karen was pretty comfortable with that. She could call the house at any time; she was never more than fifteen minutes away if she needed to get there immediately. Kenyuna had grown to an age where Karen knew that she needed some time for herself, and she did not want to be one of those smothering moms.

"Hey girl," Tasha said.

"Hey."

Tasha and Karen were doing their usual studying when Tasha said, "My brother wants to get with you; he's interested and wants to know if you want to go out with him on a date."

"Does he have a job, and what is his issue?" replied Karen.

"Girl, he's just having some hard times right now."

Karen told Tasha to have him call her, and she would think about a date later. Karen thought about it and decided it had been some time since she had been out on a date, and it couldn't hurt. One date could not hurt. They could have something in common, and if not, she could just go back to her routine with nothing lost.

Karen spoke with Donnell. He did not have a car, so Karen had to pick him up for their date. It did not sit well with her spirit, but she gave him the benefit of the doubt, knowing that life sometimes throws people into difficult situations. Even she had to get back on her feet sometimes, so she gave him a break.

What the hell, she told herself.

It had been a long time since she'd been on a date. She needed a break from the books; she made herself believe she would go have a good time, and that would be that. And that is just how it went on the date, but she did not see Donnell for a while after that. He gave her a night out, and they had a good time. She really did enjoy his company. They danced and had a few drinks, and he took her to an after-party where she met some of his friends. She could not remember the last time she had danced the night away, and she really liked his company. He did have a quality about himself that made her semi-attracted to him, or maybe she was just horny as hell. She knew she was treading on shaky ground with her emotions, so she just let them be without acting on them.

Karen and Tasha did well in the African American History class, and they became even closer friends and took more classes together. Algebra was in the distant past. Karen passed it with a grade to move on, which was a passing grade, and that was just fine with her. Tasha let her know that Donnell had moved out of her house, and she had not seen him for a while. They were not doing anything anyway. She needed to stay focused and finish with a good GPA this semester anyway. Tasha spoke nothing about her brother, and Karen did not inquire; she just had too many other things to think about right now. It was only one date. She did not know much about him, and he knew even less about her. She really did not have any attachment to him, so she honed in on her studying. As the semester was coming to an end, she thought about what she would study for the next semester. She grabbed a class schedule and headed toward the door when she heard Tasha calling her from a distance, "Wait up."

"Girl, what's up?"

"Have you decided what classes you will be taking?"

"I don't know yet, but I will call you."

"Okay. See you later."

That was the last time she saw Tasha. She tried calling her several times, but the line was disconnected. Karen hoped that she was alright, but she did not go to friends' homes without an open invitation. Also, she really did not want to run into Donnell. She thought she would see Tasha when the next semester started, which would start in a few weeks. She had already picked her new classes.

The semester started, and Tasha was nowhere to be found. She looked for weeks, hoping that she would start late. Karen just could not bring herself to drop by unannounced; maybe it was part of her southern lifestyle. Karen understood how difficult it was to be a single mother with so much responsibility on her shoulders. She prayed for Tasha and hoped that she was alright as she opened her book to the assignment written on the board. She had to get through this semester; her friend was an adult. She was sure she was handling her situation well. Summer had come again, and Karen decided she would only take two classes and give herself a little break from the full load she had been taking on. She had not heard from either guy in months, and now they were both calling. She had never been in this situation before; two guys were on her heels, and one was trying very hard to win her extra time. He became more aggressive in wanting to see her. The attention was drawing her right into a spider web that was a planned set-up that she would have to fight to get out of with her life still salvageable.

Karen thought about Donnell, whom she had met but really only knew through his sister after studying together. She really did not expect to see him again after Tasha had moved without notice. He seemed like a pretty nice guy, but something just did not sit well with her about him. Questions stuck in her mind. Why did this nice-looking brother have to live with his sister? What was his angle? Her deadline was approaching quickly, and she needed to stay focused on her final exams to get her degree. When it was finished, she could relax and think about her next moves: work a full-time job, continue her education at a four-year university, or keep working her part-time job and take a break from school for a while. She sat thinking on the balcony of her apartment when she noticed a figure riding a bicycle through her neighborhood. She took a closer look, and she could make out the body frame. It looked like Donnell, but she could not see his face. She was not sure until he got close enough for her to see his face.

"Hey girl," he called as he rode the bike onto the sidewalk and stood at the bottom of her balcony. "Can I take you out on a date?" It would be her second date with him, and her schedule was not so full now, so she agreed to go.

He still did not have a car, and Karen asked him what he was doing. He told her he had been working and had just moved into his own apartment. He told her that he was working on getting a car soon. The date was pretty fun. Donnell was a great dancer. He taught her a dance that was popular in their city, and she was a fast learner. He had all the right moves and made her feel like a woman should feel in a man's arms. She enjoyed his company, and she laughed so hard at his jokes that she could feel her mouth lines begin to hurt. He was on top of his game, and he was a professional at it. He knew exactly what to say and do. Karen only shared parts of her life with him without sharing too much of herself with a stranger.

The night lasted until early morning; she had not thought about Kenyuna at all because she knew she was safe. She was away for the weekend with her sister, and Karen was so glad that she had family here to help her in her time of need. Kenyuna loved her first cousins. They were all close in age. It was a nice break for Karen to let her hair down, knowing Kenyuna was in a safe place. Maybe she was having just as much fun with her first cousins.

Donnell called Karen regularly, asking her to come by and visit, go on an outing, or have dinner. Karen didn't think the friendship was leaning toward a relationship. She just thought it was nice to hang out with Donnell. She had too many other plans and things to do other than hang out with Donnell.

Karen told herself it would not get her where she wanted to be. She still had to be a good parent to Kenyuna, and her other time was dedicated to studying, shopping, and spending as much time as possible with other friends and relatives. She wanted to get to know the city better and do some weekend sightseeing with Kenyuna in the city. The idea of picking Donnell up to hang out with them just did not sit well with her; he still did not have a car. She had worked too hard to get a car for her and Kenyuna to ride him around town in it. She had her own agenda of things she wanted to do. Donnell was just not part of it. She just did not want that in her life right now. She was sure he did not think of them as being in a relationship. She had not spent all her time with him. She thought the feeling was mutual between the two of them. She had told him about her goals, and she would not lose focus. Donnell wanted to come over more, spend more time with her, and stay over as many nights as he could get away with. She still had this uneasy feeling that he would come over and demand her attention.

Karen wanted to be intimate with a man, and when Donnell was there, he was the lucky candidate for the moment. She knew well the difference between love and lust, and Donnell never denied her advances. He was glad to satisfy her needs.

She had not heard from Eugene, but he would be in contact with her when he wanted to be. He would call out of the blue and make plans for dinner and a movie. He was nothing like Donnell; he did not do the dancing thing at all; he was more of the conversation type, more like picking your brain on current events, etc. She shared more of her life with him. They seemed to have a lot in common in their life histories since they were close in age. He had a lot on his plate as well, and she could relate to his situation. She just did not feel that he cared for her the way she cared for him. Most of their date was just for conversation to see if they were still holding it together in life. Karen really did miss him. She didn't know how much until she saw him. He just had something about him that she really enjoyed and liked. She could see herself with him, but she could not put her finger on the reason why. There was just something between them; she could not do anything about it. She just knew they'd be friends, if not lovers, for a long time.

Karen just could not find the right opportunity to tell Donnell that she had a friendship with someone else and that she really did like him more than she could ever like him. The two relationships were so different. She enjoyed Donnell's company, but deep within, she knew she had no intention of having a long-term relationship with him. Karen knew he would not be happy with her decision. She kept it to herself. She knew he wanted a relationship with her. He talked about him moving in with her, and Karen would do what was best for her and Kenyuna. She thought about Eugene and compared the two men. She would like to get to know Eugene better. He had the qualities of a man she could enjoy being with for a long time. He had a character and personality that fit hers more closely than Donnell's. When she compared herself to Eugene, she discovered that Eugene, like her, had only one child and was divorced. He didn't do drugs or drink much alcohol, and his conversations were on a wide range of topics and levels, and she could keep up with him. They both liked to have conversations that kept them talking for hours, day or night. Karen did not want to get Eugene into any situation involving him, him, and me. She knew these types of interactions didn't work out well from her experience and others she had seen. She just was not a two-timing despicable person, nor had she ever played those types of games with people's emotions. It was just too unpredictable and new to her. She had never had to deal with two men interested in her before, so she was feeling overwhelmed.

Karen was smart enough to know that Donnell was not a stable man. She would have to get out of the situation with the least amount of damage to herself and Kenyuna. Karen did have an advantage in the situation. Donnell did not live with her, and she was glad she did not let him move in. She kept giving him excuses. She didn't really know Donnell or Eugene well. She had no serious feelings for either of them. Donnell spent more time hanging out late at night and doing drugs, although he did not do them in front of her. She knew the signs of the lifestyle of a user. She had spent many years watching her ex-husband go from husband and father to deadbeat man. She knew well the outcome of drugs and alcohol.

Karen made it perfectly clear to Donnell that she did not do drugs and did not want anything to do with that environment. She had put those things out a long time ago when she was pregnant with Kenyuna; she had something more precious to outweigh all the other stuff. She remembered when she tried to please her ex-husband by doing drugs with him and his friends, but it did not work out for him. She was not going down that road again.

Donnell came around to help with things she needed done on her car and repairs in the apartment. Yet he played on Karen's gentleness and vulnerability to get into her life. It had been several years since Karen had dated, and she had no idea that dating had changed, with pits you could fall into without knowing it until you were waist-deep in them and sinking fast. Donnell would come over and stay longer and longer until he seemed like part of the furniture. His visits would lead to spending one night, two nights, and a week together. Karen knew Donnell was there. She just had not noticed that a lot of his clothes were there if not all of them. Karen knew she would have to deal with Donnell sooner or later; he was not doing his part as a man. He could not keep a stable job; he worked washing windows between jobs. It just did not make sense to her; he did have a few clients that were on the bus route. Karen knew part of the reason he could not keep himself stable was the alcohol, and that did not sit well with her.

Karen called her sister to say hello, and as they were talking, her sister said that she had a 1983 Ford car that needed some repairs but was still drivable.

"I put a battery in it about a few months ago, and it may need a couple of tires," she said, "but you don't need to spend your money on a car. I will give it to you. It's been set in the backyard for a while, but it just might need a jump. It should start right up."

Karen was so thankful because she was sick of taking the bus to work, school, the grocery store, and wherever else she needed to go. Karen could not believe her little sister had just given her a car, something she could use right now. She had rented cars for special occasions like if she wanted to go out or take a weekend with Kenyuna sightseeing in the city. She even went out on dates with Donnell a few times in a rental car; he did not know at the time that the car was just a rental. Karen thought about how much more she could accomplish with a car. Her life would be so much easier with it.

The weekend came, and Karen and Donnell went to check the car out. She drove it home the same day. Karen could not believe that the car was drivable and was in pretty clean condition inside and out. Karen's sister signed over the title to her and wrote in a document that the car was a gift from her. It was the perfect starter car for Karen and Kenyuna. The timing was perfect. Karen and Kenyuna got acquainted so much better within the new city, and she had not put Donnell in the equation. Donnell started to stay over more often and came over early and sometimes even unexpectedly. Karen was feeling trapped. She had not felt that for a long time. In the back of her mind, she knew this would not work out between her and Donnell. She would have to take her chances with what needed to be done. It had to be done soon.

As they sat in the car after an evening outing, she told Donnell that she did not want to see him anymore. She did not love him, nor did she feel she would ever love him. She told him he needed to get his belongings out of the apartment as soon as possible. She told him that they could still be friends and that she would still be there for him.

Months later, when she and Donnell were hanging out and having dinner together, she noticed a truck coming in their direction in the distance. She knew that delivery truck and who was driving it; she could not forget and would never forget. Karen's heart dropped as she stood with her hand stuck to the car door handle as the truck drove by. She could see Eugene's face as she watched him look at her and continued to see his face from the truck's side mirror. It felt like forever as she watched the truck drive down the street and onto the next street. Donnell's voice was on mute as her eyes connected with Eugene's from the driver's mirror.

"What are you looking at?" he asked.

Karen got into the car without responding. She had not heard a word he had said. She knew she would need to make some major adjustments soon. She did not return any of Eugene's calls. She did not want him to find out this way that she was dating someone else. She did not want to discuss the situation with him for now. He knew now, and it pained her that he found out the way he did.

Karen hoped she would have Donnell all behind her, then she could be free to date whoever she wanted to without any conflicts. Donnell was like any unwanted tick: it sticks to you until it sucks blood for as long as it can until you pull it off and kill it. He was getting to be too much for her to carry; she felt like his personal cab driver at times and his mother at other times. He was just not ready or moving in the same direction as she was. It was obvious that she did not like it. Karen had earned her associate degree, and now it was time for her to move into the job market. She applied for a full-time job as the assistant manager at a retail gift shop. She really didn't know what job field she wanted to enter. She just wanted to test the field and see what she wanted to do when she got hired for the position. It was a new development in the part of the city close to downtown where she was planning on moving anyway. So the new job gave her the motivation to look for an apartment close to her new job. She decided to stay in the same area so she would not have to move Kenyuna out of the school district she was in yet. Kenyuna was already having a hard time adjusting to the fact that she had not seen her biological father for a long time. She was being asked to adjust to a new man who would never replace her father and maybe move in with them. Karen tried to make the transition as smooth as possible and noticed her little girl had grown much taller in a year. She now stood at Karen's shoulder.

Karen felt the pressure. She knew she had to do something. He would stay out late at night, getting drunk and high, then he would want to come over to her apartment or call late, disrupting her sleep. She could not deal with it anymore. She had a lot on her plate to deal with already. She was now working full-time and had other responsibilities she needed to take care of one way or another. She had to let Donnell know it was not working. He was supposed to be working, but he was mostly hanging out with his friends—people he knew from the city he had lived in all his life. He was doing stuff Karen had done years ago and in her teenage years. Her life was much different. She had herself and a teenage daughter to take care of now. The facts are that Donnell only had himself and his desires to think about and entertain. He just did whatever made him happy and what was best for him, and she felt it was at her expense.

Donnell decided to go back to washing windows around town, but she knew he was doing more hanging out around town than washing windows. Karen found the right time and nerve to tell him that things were just not working out for the both of them. He agreed to remove his things from her apartment, and that was just too easy. Karen felt uneasy about the situation but knew it was the right thing to do.

She knew it was not going to be that easy to tell Donnell it was a done deal between the two of them. Deep down, she knew she had made a big mistake by letting the situation go on for so long. She saw the same pattern from her ex-husband. She wondered why she had not recognized that pattern before now. She hoped that Donnell would just move on as she stopped contributing to his transportation needs, leaving him to get to and from his destinations by whatever means necessary. She could feel his jealousy in the air. Karen stayed away from the apartment until late so she would not have to see him or deal with him. Sometimes that worked, and sometimes it didn't because Donnell would sit at her doorstep and just wait until she came home, whenever that was. It just was not going to end as Karen had hoped. She found herself back where she was. She had tried so hard not to be depressed again. He got violent with Karen and beat her to the point where she needed to seek medical attention. She was told to place a restraining order of protection on him and file assault charges. She did just that, and even more, she lost wages and suffered distress from his immature actions. She wanted him to pay. She remembered a statement from her dear grandmother: "There is always more than one way to skin a dirty cat or dog."

Donnell tried to contact Karen to talk, but she ignored his calls or hung up the phone. After weeks of continuing to call, she finally told Donnell that it was over and that if he ever came near her or her daughter, she would kill him. Karen knew he had gotten the message loud and clear from the tone in her voice. Karen never heard from Donnell again until the appointed court date. He tried smiling at her, but she gave him the most horrible look that he didn't attempt it again. They both stood silent before the judge; not once did she ever look at him, nor did he look in her direction. It was like two strangers who never knew each other or had ever seen each other standing in front of a judge, and that was fine with Karen. The judge spoke and ordered him to pay restitution to Karen for lost wages and personal injury. Karen did not care; she just wanted this ordeal over with. She had all the support she needed from her little sister, her brother, and a family friend. She knew she would never see a dime. It was good to have him gone from her and Kenyuna's lives for good.

Several weeks later, the doorbell rang. It was the police asking to allow Donnell to get his clothes and a few other items he had left at her apartment. Karen had his things packed and was sitting at the door entranceway, which was as far as he could come inside. She did not want him any farther into her apartment. She heard the door shut, and the feeling of being trapped went out the door. She knew she would never be caught in another situation like this. She could breathe again, and she locked the door.

This new life was going to be pretty good now for her and Kenyuna, she thought to herself.

She was working every day, and Kenyuna was attending school. Winter turned into spring, and spring turned into summer, and the cycle fit her; she still felt incomplete. She just knew there was more she wanted to do. She had new friends, and she was doing a lot of different things: learning about other parts of the surrounding cities, getting lost, and having to find her way home; taking a short trip with church members; attending Kenyuna baseball and basketball games; attending teachers' conferences; and volunteering, and yet there was still something missing.

The college had reminded her how much she had missed out on the college experience. She got pregnant with Kenyuna and had to drop out to be a mother and wife. Yet she had made a vow to herself to go back and finish what she had started so long ago. She could not break that vow now; she had to continue and get her bachelor's degree. She knew it was going to take hard work and a lot of planning to accomplish it. She continued to work full-time, and now that Kenyuna was old enough to stay at home alone, she could not leave her in someone else's hands. She was a mother first, and everything else was secondary, except for God. Karen decided she would think about it and see if she could work something out that would benefit her and Kenyuna. But until that happened, she would continue on the path before her to keep life as stable as possible. Karen came to realize that life deals you a hand and that you do not have a choice other than to play the hand.

The morning started out as usual. She went to work, and Kenyuna went to school. She was called into her supervisor's office at the end of the day and was told it was her last day to work. Karen had no warning or even an idea that she would be terminated. She had never lost a job before. She had always been given notice when she would be leaving a position, but she had never been fired, terminated, or let go. Karen really enjoyed her job. She liked the contact with other people and the process of purchasing merchandise for customers she had grown to know. She enjoyed the sales work, learning the ins and outs of retail, and the income was pretty good. She earned enough to cover her monthly bills and a little bit extra for weekend fun.

The day was done. Karen went home with thoughts of how she would support herself and Kenyuna. She walked into the apartment and kicked her shoes off at the door with a heavy load on her mind about what to do next. As she walked toward the bathroom, tears streamed down her cheeks. She cried out loud from the hurt and disappointment of having to deal with all the issues in front of her now. She began to think about how her ex-husband had put her in this situation and the bad choice she had made in marrying him in the first place. She cried about being alone to raise a child without a clue of how to do it, and she cried even harder as she talked out loud that she was not supposed to be the breadwinner and financial supporter for everything. It is and has always been the man's responsibility to take care of his family; her father took care of his family. She sat on the toilet with her hands on her lap, crying. She knew Kenyuna would not be home for a few hours. She did not know how long she had been sitting there when suddenly she heard a small, still, soft voice say, "I will take care of you." Karen got up from the toilet and went to look around the apartment to see if someone had walked in, heard her crying, and spoke to her. There was no one there, so she tried to dismiss it. The voice was as clear as day. Karen dried her face, changed her clothes, and headed toward the kitchen to prepare dinner, which she had with Kenyuna. She never felt that feeling of disappointment again. She decided to get a good night's sleep and figure out what to do tomorrow. She would not tell Kenyuna that she had lost her job. She just did not want her little girl worrying about adult issues right now. Karen wanted Kenyuna to stay her little girl for as long as possible. She knew she could see her maturing physically and mentally, and in due time she would have to deal with adult matters soon enough. She knew how important the teenage years were; she just wanted her to enjoy her youth. Karen prepared for bed. Kenyuna was already asleep. She thought how nice it would be to have a good, responsible man hold her tonight, telling her that everything would be alright. If only that were the case, how easy that would be! She laid her head down and told her brain to shut up. She would have enough time to think tomorrow and work out what her next move would be.

BUTTERFLY THREE: FEELIN TRAPPED AGAIN

It had only been a few weeks. The sun was setting in the night sky. The phone rang. A familiar voice said, "Hello, and how are you doing?"

Karen could not believe her ears, but she recognized that voice. It was Eugene calling. She could not believe he had kept her phone number for that long. She had almost completely forgotten about him; she was convinced that he had forgotten about her. They talked for hours, catching up on things that had happened in their lives since the last time they talked. They even discussed the day he saw her with Donnell. He told her he made a decision not to bother her because she had made the decision to date Donnell at that time. He just did not want any more problems in his life at the time. He shared with Karen that he was going through a divorce and trying to get custody of his son. She was overjoyed that he was willing to share that part of his life with her. She felt that old connection all over again from when they first met. Before saying goodbye, Eugene made dinner plans for the weekend with her.

The conversation was nice for both of them. Eugene always picked a wonderful restaurant somewhere Karen had never been before, in a part of the city she would not go without a date. Eugene called to confirm the time a few days before. She knew it would be a long night, so she prepared her body with a nice bubble bath, some nice music, and a glass of wine. Karen checked on Kenyuna while she was waiting for Eugene's arrival. She was spending the night with her sister and little cousin. Karen trusted very few people to take care of her little girl. The doorbell rang at 7:15 p.m.; he was late, and Karen had an issue with being late, so she took her time answering the door. She did not want to seem overly excited, even though she was. She looked out to make sure it was him; she checked his outfit. He wore a nice-fitting shirt with a black jacket and slacks; everything matched. She noticed that his boots were not pointed-toe but rather round and black, which matched his jacket.

The night was starting off. The dress code was good, and the conversation flowed with ease. Dinner was great, and they shared a chocolate nonalcoholic beverage that resembled a large chocolate shake in a glass with two straws. Although Karen could taste some kind of alcohol in it, she did not let on that she knew nonalcoholic drinks from alcoholic beverages. They were both full. He asked Karen if she would not mind staying at his place tonight. He told her that he had been up late the night before and worked all day, so he was tired. She agreed to stay under the circumstances; she knew she was not anywhere near her apartment, and he lived in another state. It was late; it would take about twenty to thirty minutes to get her home, then he would have to go back home. Karen agreed.

The night had gone so well. They were both adults, and she was a grown woman. She made it perfectly clear that they would not be engaging in any sexual activity tonight. She told him to be a gentleman and sleep on his side of the bed. She would sleep on her side. She was tired too. She had a long day as well, and now, after a good meal, she could sleep well. She had no reason to distrust Eugene's words; they were his bond. He offered her a tee shirt to sleep in, and she headed toward the bathroom to change. She decided she would take a good shower the next morning before she left. She had to be out early to place an application online, and she would get dressed once she got home for the day. She got into bed. He was already there. She rolled over and pulled the covers over her to fall asleep. She felt Eugene's body next to hers when she started to doze off. An arm lay across her chest, and his hand began to rub her breast.

"What are you doing?" Karen asked.

"Come on," he said, "I want you."

"NO!"

He wasn't going to take "no" for an answer. He continued to try to be intimate with her. She was just as determined not to be intimate with him. She knew it would be a long night and hoped she would survive it. As she defended herself, the night turned into day and the sun shone into the window. What an asshole! She realized that was his plan all along; she took a deep breath. She was not going to be forced into doing something she did not want to do with him or anyone else. He must not have known she was not the same person he had met over a year ago. She was much more mature, and she was not going to be dictated to by him. She was doing what was best for her. She had learned to make her own decisions. Her no or yes was exactly what she meant. It turned out to be a night the two of them would not forget or get much sleep from. She felt good that she had stood her ground on the issue; it was time for the both of them to get up. He had very few words to say to her other than "Good morning."

He headed into the shower first, and she tried to get a nap in before it was her turn to shower. The driver was quiet. He had very few words to say to her, but the feeling was mutual. She laughed inside all the way to her apartment. He had a damaged ego.

She kissed him goodbye before getting out of his car and waved as he pulled away from her apartment building quickly. She wondered if she would ever see him again. It felt good. If you don't stand up for yourself, you will forever be falling for whatever. Last night was her test to stand up for herself. She was making changes in all areas of her life, and this was a good place to start with him. Whether it was going to work out for the better or not, she was taking a stand.

She thought about how she had made her point last night and knew it did not make Eugene very happy, but she smiled anyway. Work was not the focus. Her mind wandered off to thoughts of Eugene. Her curiosity was keeping her from doing any work today, and that night she still could not bring herself to talk with him. It was going to be hard, but she would just keep her cool and let the skeletons fall out of the closet one by one. She didn't have to wait long. She and Eugene were having an evening dinner a few weeks later at his home. The doorbell rang, and then there was a loud knock at the door. Eugene rushed to answer the door.

"I wonder who that could be," he said.

Seated at the kitchen table, she could hear a loud woman's voice coming from the doorway through the living room and echoing right into the kitchen. She got up from the table and tiptoed toward the door. The lady was trying to come inside, but Eugene told her that she was not welcome and to get off his property before he called the police. She was walking away, calling him all kinds of names. Karen heard him tell her not to ever come to his house unannounced again or he would have her arrested. She heard the door close as Eugene and the lady continued to exchange words. Karen dashed back into the kitchen and sat as if she had never left the spot she had been sitting.

"What happened?" she asked him. "Is everything alright?"

"It was nothing. Just someone I know that doesn't take no for an answer."

That answer sent a bell ringing in her head from a few weeks ago, when she had told him no and he did not want to take it as an answer. My, how the tables had turned—he found himself in the same situation she was in a few weeks ago. He said the person wanted a relationship with him, and he had told her that he was not interested. She stayed the night with Eugene, and they didn't have a conversation about the incident after that night.

Karen's thoughts raced all night in her head as she told herself she was going to dig deep to keep her peace of mind. She knew what it was like to be in a deep hole and fall in love with someone who refuses to love you back. Eugene was being very evasive. He was not sharing any of his feelings with her. She knew it would be a battle that she may or may not win. She could feel the tenderness, compassion, and fun they shared together. The evidence would come flowing out like a river running out of its bank when they shared quality time together.

She headed toward the bathroom to shower and get ready to leave for work. She would stop by her apartment to get some things for work. She noticed his trash can sitting next to the face sink, and she could not believe her eyes. There inside was an empty package of pantyhose looking right back at her. They were not the size or color she wore, and she got a loop in her throat. Her eyes became a little watery. She thought she had something special going on with this guy. She could almost picture them together for a long time, although they had not talked about being exclusive with each other. It was still a shock to her whole system. The skeletons were out of the closet, and she shouldn't be surprised. Karen composed herself and walked out of the bathroom, partially dressed. She just could not give him a pass in this situation. She waited until he came out of the shower and sat at the end of the bed where she was getting dressed.

"What's up with the pantyhose package in your trash can?" She asked.

He gave her a puzzled look after a few seconds before he spoke. She could not believe the words that were coming out of his mouth.

"Well, during the cold weather season, I wear the pantyhose for insulation and circulation to keep my legs warm and the blood flowing when I'm out on his truck route and it's really cold."

"Really now," Karen said, "so where are the lipstick, mascara, and the dress with the matching shoes? Don't you also need that to keep the rest of your body complete, all put together, and warm?"

Eugene laughed, so Karen left the subject along with the conclusion that he was full of dung. It is what it is. He was a single man with his own home, and she was just another guest, so he didn't have to explain himself to her. She needed to stay focused on her life and learn from this behavior; this was all new to her. She knew she was just another lady with a man who had been hurt by other relationships, and she was not going to be the one that saved him from hurting other women. He could have as many house guests as he can or wants. It was his world, but she was not going to play along with him, and he was not going to play her.

She felt foolish and embarrassed. She and Eugene continued to dress, and she dressed even faster. She knew things would never be the same and could feel the tears building up inside. If she was not careful, they would soon be flowing out. She would not let him see the hurt he had caused her; she really had hoped that he had come back into her life to start a long-term friendship. She was just not looking for games anymore, especially with her emotions. This was deeply disappointing to her. She drove and cried. When she pulled into the parking lot, she cleaned her face. She would deal with the situation she had found herself in later.

She kept her distance for a few weeks and did not take any of his calls; she let the answering machine catch them because she knew he would be calling. She decided that it was time to depend on herself. She would work on herself, and to hell with any man for now. With her thoughts in check, she returned all the calls left on her answering machine with a new purpose and a new attitude.

Fall was here again, with leaves falling from the trees. Karen looked for a part-time job. She decided to go to college full-time. She had spent three years as an assistant manager; she really liked that job and missed it too, but it was time to move on and get on with what she wanted to do. She also missed the little volunteer ladies; they were so easy to work with. She had thoughts about returning to college long enough. She dropped out once, but that was not going to be the case again. She had nothing holding her back this time; her world was not spinning out of control. She was standing on her own two feet. She would put herself first and go for it. Kenyuna was in middle school, and she could pretty much take care of herself. She trusted her to stay home in the evening for a few hours without her. She seemed to be a good young lady with no disruptive behavior. She didn't talk back, yell, or scream. Karen felt she was doing something right and that it was a good time to finish college. It was either now or never. She would take some classes to brush up on some courses she knew she didn't like, like algebra. She knew there would be some type of placement test to get into the university. It had been a year since she had gotten her associate's and helped Kenyuna with her homework assignment. She learned some new stuff, but that was not going to be enough. She signed up for two evening classes during the week and found a part-time job that worked around her schedule.

She continued to see Eugene and realized he was not ready for a serious relationship with her or anyone else. He had made that perfectly clear to her, and she thought maybe she was not ready for a serious one either. She thought about how nice it would be to be able to do whatever she wanted only having to answer to God and Kenyuna. It was okay with her.

She could not believe how fast the time had passed. Kenyuna was going to graduate from high school soon. Karen could not be more proud of what Kenyuna had achieved. She was a happy mom. Her daughter had achieved what 72 percent of high school youth do not. She would make the graduation one that she would never forget. Whatever she wanted, Karen would work hard to make it happen. Kenyuna wanted her dress made, not store-bought, and she wanted a rental car for the whole weekend. Kenyuna asked if she could stay out all night with her friends for the first time in her young life. Karen would have to give that some consideration and was thankful for the time she had to do so.

Kenyuna was still very young. Although she had accomplished a lot, she was still Karen's baby girl, and she would not take any chance of letting her hurt herself or anyone else. Karen knew what prom nights meant and what could happen in one fun-filled night. The excitement could end with a lifetime of sorrow and shame. Karen would take all precautions to prevent any dangerous situation for her little girl's life at this time. She was still the responsible parent, and she would act like it even during this exciting time for her and Kenyuna. Kenyuna was on her A game. She had all her plans together. She knew who she wanted to make her dress, and she had about two months to pull this graduation off. She called and made arrangements for the rental car. She only had to put the deposit down, set the available dates, and pay. Karen remembered her graduation experiences and was determined to make

Kenyuna's graduation day as memorable as possible so that one day she would share her graduation experiences with her daughter.

Karen was proud that she had gone to the basic education class and gotten her GED—better late than never. She was setting an example for her daughter. She thought of how she only needed a few credit points in high school to complete it and how easy that would have been to do. She wanted to see the world; she did not think that getting her diploma was that important at the time. She smiled to herself at the promise she had kept to herself. She had now gotten her high school diploma and had a two-year degree. She looked over the schedule from the university she had picked up on her way to the office. She was actually going to attend this university in the fall.

BUTTERFLY FOUR: WHERE DID THE TIME GO?

Who said time doesn't heal old wounds? Only if you don't have something to do it with or to keep you preoccupied. Karen got out of bed on a slow morning with nothing pressing to do. Her mind began to wonder how much she had accomplished in such a short length of time without much support from anyone she could count on. She thought deeply about things, realizing she did not have much support financially from Eugene or her ex-husband. She had gotten all this way on her own merits. Karen wanted to complete college before she was too old, lost interest, or just settled for whatever life would offer her. The time was now. She promised herself—a promise is just that, and this one she had made to herself long ago, she would keep. She didn't have a clue, but she would cross that bridge when she got to it today.

It was the first thing on her mind when we woke up that morning. She dressed for the day and moved around the apartment, trying to be as quiet as possible to let Kenyuna sleep. During the week, her baby girl gets up so early to catch the school bus. The weekend she deserved to sleep in as long as she wants today. They both did not get home after 6:00 p.m. and were up again at 6:00 a.m., which was early since they went to bed late.

Months had passed, and thoughts of Eugene crossed her mind. She missed and loved their conversations, which were never boring. She felt their communication was good between them in a competitive kind of way. He still played his little tricks with her, and she just played along with them. Karen did something that turned the tides for the both of them forever, never to return, and tricks had come to a squeezing stop. Karen answered his phone while he was not home, and lo and behold, there was another female voice on the other end. Karen told the caller that Eugene was not available and asked if she could take a message.

The voice said, "No, I'll call back later."

She didn't tell him of the call once he returned home. He got another call and left again, leaving Karen there alone. She knew in her heart and spirit that it was the end for her and Eugene; it was well with her. The player got played. It was days, if not weeks when it hit the ceiling. He was mad at her, so he let her have it.

"When I come to your house, I don't answer your phone," he said, "nor do I walk around your home looking in your things. As a guest at someone else's home, I get somewhere and sit down."

He told her that she was totally wrong for doing that and asked her why she had done it. Karen said it was a natural thing for her to do being that she answered her phone at home; she had forgotten that she was not at home. He did not buy that story; he told Karen that their relationship was done and he did not want to see her anymore. Tricks are for kids, but that was just fine with her; she had other things to accomplish anyway. She found out what she needed to prove that he was just a trickster. He was not being honest with her and was not being upfront with her. She was headed on another journey in her life.

She enrolled in the university, fulfilling a promise she had made to herself a long time ago. It would help her self-esteem, help her get over him, and keep her as busy as possible. Slowly and surely, the twelve to fifteen credit hours per semester did just that. He became the last thing on her mind, which kept her from thinking about the lies and secrets he would have kept telling her. He also had issues that preoccupied his time. His son was very important to him. He had been trying to get custody of his son from his ex-wife for several years. He really didn't have much time to spend with her the way she wanted it to be between them.

It had been close to a year, and she had practically forgotten about him. But never say never; she was studying for an exam the next day when the phone rang. She tried to ignore it and let the answering service pick it up, but she answered it anyway.

"Hello, how are you?"

"I'm fine, and how are you?"

Karen felt like it had only been a couple of months since she had heard that voice. It had been almost a year. They talked for a long time until he asked her if he could take her out for dinner and a movie. She said yes, she could use a break or time-out from the books. She knew she would have a good conversation with him if nothing else. She wanted the opportunity to spend some time with him to catch up on his life. She had not met too many new friends to share her time with in a year. She and Eugene had something that you just don't find every day with all the people that you encounter. They could always have a conversation of interest with each other, and it was easy in his company. She remembered a phrase that went something like this: "Never burn the bridge that one day you might have to cross back over again." She would keep her newfound friend.

Wayne was one of the good guys, and there was no pressure from him to ask for anything she did not want to give. He often invited her to concerts and musical outings as a guest. He was some kind of promotion director for the arts at this company. They discussed what concerts or musicals were in town, and he would ask her to come with him. Sometimes she would accommodate him, but most of her time was spent with Kenyuna and her study schedule. She made time to hang out with Eugene if she was not with Wayne. Sometimes she would not return either of their calls at all. She met Wayne a few months earlier while taking some classes. He was a volunteer. She was impressed by that, and he flirted with her. She could not figure out why an attractive young man would be spending his time assisting people to get their GED, studying for a college student like her who was just updating their skills. He was very attentive to her, and he took the time to explain the questions that she did not understand about geometry and calculus, which were taboo to her. It had been a long time since she had had these classes. He occasionally invited Karen out for a social cocktail and dinner, and she accepted once or twice. She really did enjoy his company, and his sense of humor made him attractive. She did not feel any sparks flying. They just were not there. He was fun to hang out with, and maybe he would grow on her. She could see herself dating him, but the thought of intimacy was out of the question. She was not attracted to him.

She continued to accommodate him on dates around the city, which gave her a better insight into what the city had to offer her. Spring was leaving, and winter was fast approaching. She knew she would have a hard time keeping her focus during the winter months. The winter had always been a challenge for her mental state. The days became shorter, and the darkness came earlier, which made her physically tired. She was not going to limit herself to waiting on anyone to validate her decisions. She would date and be a lot more selective in her choices from now on. Their friendship was just what it was. She would live her life, and he would live his. They got together and had a good time, and if not, it was well with her.

Wayne called early, asking her out to lunch. He said he wanted to talk to her about something. She wondered the rest of the day what it could be; they had been hanging out for almost a year now. She knew her busy schedule, and she knew he traveled a lot. He promoted concerts coming into the city and wrote a review column for a grassroots local paper. He told her that he was leaving and moving back to his hometown. He said he needed to be closer to his son and be a father now that his son was getting older. Karen understood and told him that she thought that was the best thing for him to do and that more fathers should stay in their children's lives like he was doing. He was doing what a man and a father should do. He paid his child support, and he visited his child, especially during the long summer months. He worked long days and long hours to visit his son on the holidays and long weekends. He wanted to get to know his son, and he wanted his son to get to know him.

If she had to choose one of the many guys she dated over the years, Wayne would have been the one to keep and not the one that got away. She was going to miss him deeply and could feel the hurt already. He took time to enjoy her company, and he shared his life with her. She learned from him how a man should treat a woman. He always made her feel like she was the center of his attention. She never felt out of place among his colleagues or friends. He was the most sensitive, caring, and attentive person Karen had ever met. He scored high on her scale of male friends that she had met in a long time. His touch was gentle, and his hands were soft. He sat close to her and made her feel safe. She thought the reason she enjoyed him so much was that he never demanded anything from her. His patience was exceptional. If she allowed him to kiss her, it was not forced or demanded. She felt comfortable with him. They had dinner or breakfast when they spent time together listening to music or hanging out. He often worked from home, making arrangements for concerts. Spending hours on the phone was his job, and he was good at getting things done. Karen realized that she and Wayne had not been intimately involved sexually, and neither he nor she was pushing the issue. He had to be having sex with someone if he wasn't having sex with her. She enjoyed his company whenever they hung out, and that was that.

"Karen, don't do it," a voice shouted in her head, but she did it anyway. Karen began to look around his apartment while he was in the shower. She just could not understand how a handsome-looking, well-groomed, clean-cut guy had not approached her to be sexual with her. She found what she was looking for as she lay on the bed with her thoughts. It was a long strand of hair. It was not the color or texture of hers. She felt betrayed and a little disappointed, yet she was not shocked. She was more relieved that he was not gay. She actually smiled. He was getting his sexual gratification from someone, at least. She really didn't care that he was having sex with someone else. She really felt relieved; she did not want to damage their relationship with sex when it was not there, to begin with. Their relationship continued as if there was no difference. The love they shared was special, and nothing could replace it. At times, she felt that he wanted more from her, but she could not bring herself to cross that line. She just never had a greater friendship with any man without having to give something in return to keep him interested in being with her.

She continued to date both Wayne and Eugene around her school schedule and Kenyuna time. She thanked God for her sister. She often helped her with Kenyuna when her schedule got too busy for her some days. Karen kept her focus on completing school and taking care of Kenyuna. She enrolled in several American history classes and found them to be very interesting. She learned so much about her heritage and the history of her ancestors that she never knew about. She enrolled in as many as she could because it would shape her life for many years to come.

Most classes had all Caucasian teachers, and she would have to prove herself to them for sure. In her last semester, things would change. The instructor for this semester was a young, brown-skinned male teacher. He sat at the desk, waiting for all the students to enter the room. Karen sat a few rows back, just in view, to see everything. She opened her book and occasionally looked at the handsome man behind the desk. Not very often had she seen a brown-skinned male teacher in the years she had been in college. Every once in a while, he would catch her looking at him, and they would have a moment of eye contact. She would drop her head down and continue to scan the book in front of her. She was excited with the materials she saw while scanning the book and felt she would do well in this class. Attendance was complete, and the introductions of the students and why we all wanted to take this class were out of the way.

Mr. K. passed out his agenda; she felt this would be one of her easier classes. She could spend more time studying for the algebra class, which was going to be a challenge. It had been a long time since she had taken any of the math classes she would need to graduate.

A few weeks had gone by. The history class was just what Karen needed. It was funny, exciting, and interesting. He would challenge her to think outside the box and see that all things you read, saw, and heard should be investigated before you take them as truth. A lot of history was not all black and white; most people don't know black people put black people on the ships that brought them to American shores. It's all written about how black people really got here and what happened once they got there. Mr. K's classroom became a common pastime for her and other classmates. She enjoyed it.

She wanted more of what Mr. K knew about history that she had not heard until now. She learned as much of it as possible while she could. Mr. K revealed that he was not from this area and that he did not know very many people in the city.

He would invite some students to have lunch with him in the cafeteria, then go and watch the school football or basketball game after school hours. She was attracted to Mr. K, and she felt the feeling was mutual. He seemed to enjoy her company as much as she enjoyed his. She attended some of the after-school activities with other students.

She sat next to Mr. K that day. He asked her if she would like to have dinner with him. She justified her action and his action by saying that he is an adult man and she is an adult woman, so whatever they did off campus was not anyone else's business. She accepted his invitation to dinner at his apartment. Their children were mature young ladies now. Also, neither had any attachments. They both knew the consequences if anyone found out that a professor was having sexual intercourse with a student. That did not stop them from crossing the line between professor and student. Mr. K did not feel threatened by his action or that any harm would come from the relationship they shared. She enjoyed the sex for as long as it lasted. It was just a physical attraction; it would not last forever. Mr. K shared his plans to return to his hometown soon with her. He was seeking a professor's tenure at a university near his hometown. His family was there, his child was there, and his mother and father were there. He only needed a few semester hours on his dissertation to complete it. She told herself to stay focused and stay on the task she had set for herself. She could and would walk away just like she had her ex-husband and the others after.

That seemed like so long ago now that she gave it some thought that she could not believe that it had been so long ago. She realized that she would be graduating soon. She had to start thinking about how she would rearrange her schedule to accommodate Kenyuna's prom while keeping a roof over their heads without losing her sanity in the process. The time drew near to complete Mr. K's class. He encouraged her to continue her education and even pursue a higher degree. His encouragement was well received and placed in the back of her mind that day. She had learned that the higher the degree, the less the government would aid her financially. She would be paying for higher education for the rest of her life. Her GPA was not great, but she decided to walk with the graduating class anyway. She said her goodbyes to the teachers who had inspired her to move on. She appreciated the full experience of college even at her age; she enjoyed the atmosphere of hanging out with younger people; thinking that she could have been a big sister, maybe a stepmother to some. She was sad because after all her achievements; she knew she would never see Mr. K again. He would be in her memories for a long time while she moved on with her life's journey.

When Kenyuna was older and ready for college, she would encourage her to go to college so she could enjoy all the excitement, hard work, and fun that came with it. Karen knew that her life would never be the same, so she embraced its fullness and looked forward to the challenges ahead. Her GPA was good enough for her to be accepted into the university to which she had applied. She made the appointment to see the counselor, and with hope and a lot of prayers, it would work out. Her nervousness was all over the place as she waited for her name to be called. Ms. Thompson was her name in the student counselor's office. She sat behind a big desk, looking over Karen's documents. Karen held her breath and waited. Ms. Thompson looked up in her direction and said, "Ms. Karen, please sit. We can take all of your credits. You will only need about sixty credits more to complete your degree with us."

Karen could not believe her ears.

"Thank you!"

She enrolled in the classes that day for the following semester. She could not wait to tell someone about the good news. She was as high as she had ever been in her life. She had never felt this kind of high when she experimented with illegal drugs. She called Poole. They had taken a few classes together and kept in touch with each other. She asked him about the outcome of his meeting with his counselor and if everything went well for him. It did not turn out well for him; they did not take all his classes, so they would not have a lot of classes together. She put the thought out of her mind as she walked toward her car. She could not wait to share the news with Kenyuna. She wanted to tell him her good news, so she just listened to him and told him she would call him later. She knew that anyone would be happy for her, especially Kenyuna.

She hadn't spoken to or heard from Poole for over two weeks. She knew that he worked a lot of odd hours. She called his cell phone but got no answer. She refused to call his home. He lived with his girlfriend, so she kept her distance from that situation. She knew that was off limits, so she waited until he called her or she saw him on campus. The phone rang. It was Poole calling her from his job.

"Hey, Girl. Did you get in?"

"Hey, Poole. Yes, did you?"

"Yes."

"How did it go? What classes are you taking?"

"Criminal Justice."

"I'm doing the Sociology program."

"Okay, I'm at work, so I've got to go."

"I will see you on campus in a few weeks."

"OK, bye-bye," Karen said. "Talk with you later."

She really did get a break this time since all her credit transferred toward her degree. She learned that only twenty-five of Poole's credits transferred toward his degree. She was sad for him because he would have to take more than forty credit hours to get his degree, and by then she would have graduated. She hoped that she and Poole would walk down the aisle on graduation day, which looked like it was not going to happen. They had classes and studies together before she would miss him dearly. She found they would not have any classes together, but they still supported one another when they could.

They found time in their busy schedules to have breakfast or lunch together to catch up on what was going on in each other's lives. But the demands on both their schedules only permitted them to see each other every few weeks.

University classes were different; they required a lot more assignments and tests, and multitasking was a necessary skill. If you did not have that skill, you were in big trouble. Karen found that assignments had deadlines and due dates with no exceptions. You either completed it or you failed the class. She did not want to repeat classes, so she put a deadline on herself long before she got there.

BUTTERFLY FIVE: GETTING TO KNOW "ME"

They went out on a weekend for the first time in a long time. Eugene did not have to work. Karen needed to study, but she could not resist the invitation to an outing with him. She could also bring Kenyuna along for the day. The outing was just what she needed—a good day to let her hair down and enjoy Eugene. He was a real gentleman; he brought his camera along, taking pictures of the sites they visited and pictures of Kenyuna and her. He would call out of the blue to see if she would like to hang out with him on the weekends when he did not have his son. This weekend, it worked out that Kenyuna had no plans for the weekend. It gave her the perfect opportunity to see how Eugene would interact with her. Previously, they had little to no contact with each other. Eugene was not her father. She was still hurting from the separation from her biological father. It turned out to be a great day hanging out with Eugene. He gave Kenyuna as much attention as he gave Karen. The ride was quiet as Kenyuna sat looking out the window toward the sites she saw. She was anxious to see an art museum on a cold but sunny day. The day went smoothly, and she seemed to enjoy the outing. They seemed comfortable being around each other. The day was a memorable one.

Karen felt the relationship game had taken a chunk out of both of their sails. They were just content with being close friends. They stuck to conversations over the phone, maybe an outing every now and then, and that was just fine with the both of them. Karen still had school to finish, and he was in the middle of a court battle with his ex-wife. She still found their conversation stimulating. He loved to debate with her in conversation on all types of subjects. Although their outing was limited, she returned his call whenever he called. They spent as much time together as could be tolerated and when her schedule permitted. Eugene had his caring ways that she liked about him, and before she knew it, a half year had come and gone. She was still not ready to be intimate with him or anyone else. She still had a lot on her plate to figure out about herself. Her mind was to stay close to Kenyuna and help guide her through these dangerous times for a teenager while trying to finish college as soon as she could. She did not want to spend another year in college without a clue of what she wanted to complete by the next year.

She had plans to have dinner with Eugene. He picked the place and time and would get back to her. The Orchard Restaurant was a great place. It was romantic, elegant, classic, and quiet. They ate dinner, and she felt compelled to share parts of her life history with him. She told him about Donnell, whom she had dated and who had beaten her up. She talked about her ex-husband, who became a drug addict and abandoned her and Kenyuna. She shared how she felt right then—she loved being single, but she preferred being married. He just listened without interrupting her. He was that kind of guy; they were both dealing with life, and sometimes it was messy. She felt they had a lot in common. Their stories were very comparable.

Dinner was done. He asked Karen if she would like to come to his house tonight. She declined because she still had a lot of studying to do for a test the next day. He understood. She knew he did not like being told no, but it did not bother her. He drove her to her apartment in silence as the music played on the radio. A goodnight kiss on the cheek ended the night, as they both told each other they would call later. She knew it would be a while before he would call. His ego was a little damaged, but he would have to get over it. He would find another way to get her where he wanted her to be before he would call again.

"Hello."

"Hi, stranger."

"I really did enjoy the dinner date. The restaurant was a good choice." If he was trying to impress her, he had done a good job.

"How would you like to go out to dinner this weekend?"

No, he did not just ask me out to dinner again.

Red flags went up like a red light. The hair on the back of her neck stood up. He was not the type of guy who would take you out to dinner twice without wanting something in return. What he didn't know was that Karen had her share of experiences dating several guys. All types of guys and her ex-husband had really taught her well. Her father had told her about all the types of guys she would come into contact with, what most of them wanted, and how they would try any means necessary to get it. She had dates with guys with money who wanted to buy their way in, ones without money who wanted to play their way in, fast talkers, liars, and cheaters. She knew he did not know what she knew, so she would just go along with what he had on his mind.

Eugene decided they should share a drink. He ordered a chocolate margarita mix that they shared. She drank her share. Why not? It was a special occasion. It was only one drink, and the occasion may not come around again. She could feel the alcohol in her system. It felt warm inside. She smiled across the table at him, and he smiled back. He said it was getting late and that he did not want to drive after the drink they had shared. He suggested she stay at his house, being that it was the closest to drive to. She told him that she had to pick Kenyuna up pretty early the next morning from her sister's house. He insisted. He did not want to drive this late since he had been drinking alcohol, which he normally doesn't do. She conceded and told him that she would stay but that she would sleep on the couch. She knew that she did not want to be intimate with him, and she just was not comfortable with him after their last encounter over the phone call incident. She respected him for letting her know that he was not able to drive in his condition. She decided that maybe it was a good idea to stay at his house for the night. She felt pretty comfortable. The drink had helped her relax after a long week of class assignments and work. She knew she would fall asleep in no time because the alcohol had taken its toll on her system. She decided she would sleep in bed with him and explain to him that she would not be intimate with him.

He didn't understand that no is no, and she couldn't understand why. She began to fall asleep, so she shifted her body into the right position to call it a night. His hands rubbed her back all the way down to her butt and then slowly back up. She pushed his hands down, but he was not having it. He moved closer to her. She pushed him back and moved as close to the edge of the bed as she could. She knew she was on his territory, and she would have to play really carefully in this situation. He seemed to be determined to be intimate with her, but she was just as determined to not be intimate with him. The night was a rollercoaster ride. They rolled, turned, flipped, and laughed most of the night.

When the day came, both got maybe a few hours of sleep as the sunlight was blasting through the blinds. He got out of bed first. He did not like what his night had been like, based on the expression on his face. He had to go to work without much sleep. It was going to be a long day for him. She had the day off, so she had plans to sleep a few hours before she would get Kenyuna from her sister's house. She had forgotten to get a towel before getting into the shower. She called out to him, "Can I get a towel, please?"

The door cracked open, and he placed a towel on the toilet for her. She could feel the tension in the air as he closed the door quietly. She dried off and put her clothes on quietly. He sat at the table eating breakfast when she came from the shower. She could hear no sounds or noises.

The drive was quiet. She didn't even know if she would ever see him again. She hoped that would not be the case. If that would be the turning point in their relationship or friendship, so be it. She would not let anyone else dictate to her what she wanted to do and did not want to do. Being sexually intimate in a relationship with him or any man would be on her terms. She would not be undermined or manipulated into doing anything she didn't want to do ever again. She really did not expect him to call again. She had really buried his ego pretty well. It was going to take some time for him to process. She was her own woman now, and she did not need him to tell her that was a fact.

It had been about a week or more later when she got a call. She was surprised at the voice on the other end of the phone. He had gotten over his ego, and he still wanted to see her, whenever that would be. She was working her schedule like a pro. She did not skip a beat. She took morning classes and worked a part-time job in the evenings. Kenyuna was adjusting to her surroundings and meeting new friends at school and in the neighborhood.

Eugene was working a lot of overtime to get custody of his son, and he was paying for the lawyer. He had to do it for his child, and she understood that in some situations, one parent is better to raise children. He said he could do a better job at parenting and raising his child. Maybe there was some other reason for him wanting custody, but she did not inquire. She knew how sensitive parents are about their children, especially when money is involved. She could not say what the truth was. She had her own issues to deal with. She hoped things would work out for him in the end. He often talked about his ex-wife and what she had done to him, but she knew there were always two sides to a story. She often listened and did not say many words. She recalled her own marriage and how love can go from sweet to bitter. She was sure her ex-husband felt the same way about her.

Eugene felt the need to express his feelings to her so she would keep an open mind and not be judgmental or too hard on him. He was going through a difficult divorce. In her mind, she knew she would be doing the same thing soon. She had not shared with him that part of her life story. Her time would come soon enough that she would need a listening ear. She did not remember her divorce being this difficult. Her ex-husband did not have a clue where she was. She would do it without his consent. She hit the books hard and was determined to finish college while she was still young. She could not waste any more time worrying about other people's problems and concerns. She had not forgotten that she was still a parent first to Kenyuna; everything else was secondary.

The day started out regular, with nothing pressing, but by the evening, things would bring the light a little closer to home. Karen and Eugene would have an evening alone, just hanging out and doing nothing stressful, with a little dinner at his house and watching a movie with a lot of conversations going on. It was about 9:30 p.m. when the doorbell rang. She wondered who it could be.

"Who is it?" He said, as he got up from the table and headed toward the door.

Karen heard the door close behind him as the voices rose to a disturbing level. She moved closer toward the door area so she could hear what was going on.

"Don't you ever come to my house again uninvited; get off my FUCKIN' property."

"I'm coming in."

"No, you are not, and if you do not leave now, I will call the police."

Karen saw the handle of the door move, and she ran back to the kitchen table as if she had been there all the time. From the outside, in the distance, she could hear a car door slam and the engine of a car start.

"Who was that?" Karen asked him as he sat back at the table.

"Just someone who does not know how to take no for an answer." She had learned how to leave well enough alone, so she moved on to another conversation. He cooked dinner, and Karen felt compelled to at least do the dishes as he watched something on the TV. She sat next to him on the couch. He seemed to enjoy her closeness to him. The doorbell rang again, and he got up to answer it once more. Karen was even closer to the door this time when he stepped outside the door and closed it. She jumped up and stood right next to the door.

"What do you want? I told you that I did not want you; what part of that do you not understand? Now leave my property."

"Get your hands off me."

"Get off my property."

"I'm going to call the police if you don't take your hands off me."

Karen put her hands over her mouth; the conversation was now louder than it was before. She was sure he knew she could hear what was going on and being said. He did not know that she had a front-row seat. The doorknob turned, and she ran to the couch and sat as if nothing bothered her. He was angry, and it showed from the expression on his face that his mood changed. Karen did not press the issue. She did not say anything at all about what she had just heard.

He said he was sorry about that situation; the person at the door was trying to make him be with her after he told her no.

Karen's thoughts ran wild. She knew what that was all about. She had worn those shoes before. She had been on the receiving end before, and it did not turn out well at all. She knew this would not be the end of his problem with this person. She decided to just get through the evening, make the most of it, and get home safely. Things quieted down; no more uninvited guests came as they settled in to enjoy sports and a movie. The evening was getting late. She needed to get going. She had a couple of classes early in the morning. She still needed to pick up Kenyuna from her sister's house. She felt he did not want her to go as he kissed her and held her close.

"Can you stay tonight?" He whispered in her ear.

She could never resist him. Her mind said no, but her body, which was close to his, said yes. She called her sister to see if Kenyuna could stay overnight.

"Hello, Yvonne, can Kenyuna stay overnight? I will pick her up first thing in the morning."

"Okay girl, you know she will be okay here."

"Thanks."

The lovemaking was just what both of them needed. He never disappointed her.

***

Morning came quickly, sooner than she wanted it to. She could hear the shower running, and she rolled over to find an empty bed. She cleared her mind and walked toward the bathroom.

What a night! She thought as she sat on the toilet; she would not have another one like this for a while. She was getting too old for this stuff. She needed to stay focused on what she had to do and what was going to be good for her future. She jumped in the shower, passing him on the way out.

"Good morning."

"Hey."

She closed the door and let the water run over her body. The steam refreshed her mind. He was all dressed by the time she got out of the shower.

"Did you have a good night's sleep?" he asked, touching her.

"Yes, it was good."

She continued to dress, finding her clothes all over the bedroom. She started to stuff what she didn't wear in her bag. She had to get going. She had a lot to do this morning. Her first class started at 9:30 a.m. He called her from downstairs and told her that it was time to go. He did not want to be late for work. She ran to kiss him while heading toward the door. She had several stops to make along the way. The distance from his house to her apartment was not just around the corner. The good thing was that the traffic would not be bad that early in the morning. She would take advantage of that and take some shortcuts around the city she had become familiar with. She picked up Kenyuna and stopped at the apartment. She dropped her bag down on the floor and ran a comb over Kenyuna's hair. It looked good enough to let it go for today with a little jelly around the edges. When you are a parent, you learn to multitask without even thinking. It's something a woman can do without even thinking about it. This applied to most single women she knew, but not all. She focused on her schooling and Kenyuna.

When it dawned on her that she had not spoken with Eugene, it had been weeks. Although that was not unusual for their relationship, it seemed strange that he had not called her; he could be just as busy as she was. She felt something was going on but could not put her finger on it. She called him for two days straight but continued to get the answering machine. She tried a few more times and decided after that she would leave it alone. She assumed that he was working overtime and spending the rest of his time with his son.

She understood that taking care of children was a full-time job. Another week passed, and she had this uneasy feeling in her spirit that she could not shake. She chose to just wait for him to call and hope that all was well with him. Karen was just about at the point of accepting that he was an absent friend, lover, or whatever when the phone rang. It was him.

"Hello," his voice came through the phone.

"Hi, what's up?"

"You won't believe what has happened to me."

"What?" she asked.

"I have been in jail."

"What?"

"Remember that incident at my house awhile back when someone came to the house?"

"Yes."

"Well, that person filed rape charges against me, and I was arrested for rape. I have been in jail for a few days, working with a lawyer to get the charges dropped, and he bonded me out of jail."

Karen could have fallen to the floor; she knew that the situation was not over and would not end well. She felt sorry for Eugene for being in that situation, but she did not feel that sorry for him. She recalled a saying her grandmother told her when she was a young lady: "Everything that looks good may not be good for you." Those words rang in her ears like chapel bells. You play games with people's emotions when your intentions are not good, which is why the outcome could end up being TROUBLE. She knew his plate was full with the rape changes (no joke), the custody battle with his ex-wife (no joke), and working full-time. Whatever time he had left in his schedule, it would be very little for her, and that was cool with her. She had her own issues. Her plate was just as full; little did he know.

"I will get with you later," he said.

She knew that could be weeks or even months from now. She could not waste any time wondering when, how, where, or if he would get back to her. She left the conversation feeling at peace; at least he was okay under the circumstances. She was glad that he had shared his concerns with her. She could now put her mind at ease and move forward. She knew he was handling the situations the best way he knew how. Karen knew he was in for a long fight and hoped it would work out for him somehow. Rape charges are not something you take lightly. He did not call as often as she would like him to. She understood his need to focus on his situation.

She knew that in most rape cases, a person could end up in prison for life. Even though he did not express his worry in his voice, she knew he was under a lot of pressure. He did not fool her, and although you can fool some people some of the time, you cannot fool everybody. She determined in her mind that the lack of contact over the next few weeks spoke a volume of words without him telling her. She knew how it felt to outstay your welcome in a city; maybe it was time for him to move on.

He had lived in this city all his life, and he had made this woman very unhappy and angry with him. And there is nothing like a scorned woman, and there is nothing she will not do to get back at you. Karen had seen his pattern and noticed that it was his way or the highway, and he had many issues. He loved the fact that he owned his home, had a great job, was a single man, was handsome, and had confidence in himself. So if you came his way, you would have to dance to his tune, or you better have your shit together or a game plan for yourself. She knew the pain and sadness that came with the divorce, and she would not wish it on her worst enemy. It takes a long time to get over the loss of love, especially the one you loved for so long and don't anymore. Karen kept on her course and thought about the pain and heartaches she had just begun to heal from herself. She said a prayer for him that his clouds would not last long and the sun would soon shine for him. She knew that when you are hurt, there are very few words that anyone can say to you at a time. She knew that the best thing to do was to let him deal with it in his own way. She would be as supportive as he would allow her to be. Her resolve was to let the situation run its course and continue to do what was best for her and Kenyuna. That would be her main focus and concern now, and she hoped that she would hear from him soon.

BUTTERFLY SIX: DON'T BE AFRAID TO CATCH OTHER BUTTERFLIES

She was learning how to live her life and enjoying the fruit of her hard labor for the first time in years. Things were finally looking good, and she was feeling good. She felt like she was lying on a bed of roses, even if it was in her mind. She had just finished her first degree after changing her mind twice. She decided she would just study whatever she wanted to and see what she found interesting. She started with American history and African American history; she even tried a music class in which she could not catch up with the notes as fast as some of the younger students in the class. She passed it with a grade that was not that great. Physical education was a class she took just to get her mind clear for the next stage of her education, which worked out pretty well for her. She was looking good and feeling good. By the time the semester had come to an end, she had dropped classes that did not hold her interest while excelling in others. She had a total of sixty or more credit hours under her belt to complete her degree. She met all kinds of people who were great additions to her life.

Mr. Poole was one of those people that she needed in her life, and he came along at the right time. She would never forget him. He was a quiet kind of guy. Most women would look right over him if they looked at him at all. They became good friends after taking a lot of classes together. He had come back to school after leaving his job. It required all police clerks to have a degree. She was doing something that she had promised herself she would do a long time ago after she found out she was pregnant with Kenyuna many years ago. It was a promise to herself, not to her parents or because all her classmates had gone on to college. She really did want to attend college in the future, just not right after high school. Her plans changed dramatically. She had to work on her darling daughter's plan. Karen did not want to be pregnant and did not expect to get pregnant by her ex-husband. She just wanted to explore and have a little fun hanging out with the wrong friends, staying out late at night, and coming home if she wanted to or not. She was doing stuff in her twenties that her parents didn't approve of. She was just letting her wings out before she would become a pillar in society, get a job, make some money, and start college. That was her plan, but she found out that plans don't always work out the way you want. Her plans didn't change. However, she kept her promise, even if it was delayed a few decades.

In algebra class, Mr. Poole's desk was right across the way from hers. She introduced herself and settled in for the instructions for the assignments. She invited him to have lunch with her, knowing she would need him for this algebra class. She purposely took Algebra II last time. It was not one of her stronger subjects, and it would take all the help she could get to pass it. They talked for an hour about their lives and why they were attending college at their age. She felt good having someone in her age bracket attend college with her. She could relate to him, and she felt she was talking to someone who understood her. She soon realized that college had no age limit. Its campus population could range up to and over her age. She took all her classes during the midday hour and worked in the afternoon part-time. It was an excellent schedule for her and Kenyuna's lifestyle.

She shared with Mr. Poole how she had lost her job as a gift shop assistant manager a while ago and how much she really liked that job. She told him she found herself not knowing what she was going to do at one time. She shared with him that she actually enjoyed purchasing merchandise, and the customers often told her that she had an eye for what they liked. She purchased items that she would buy for herself and wear herself. She knew what ladies liked and was learning what men liked as well. She got to know some customers on a personal level, and they would ask her to purchase more quality merchandise. They shared with her that it had been a long time since they had good merchandise in the shop that drew them to come to the shop. She was getting compliments from customers on how the gift shop had not looked that good or had this kind of quality merchandise for years. Karen felt really good, even if she did not know some of them by name. She took the compliments anytime. She had learned to go with the flow; if it's not broken, don't change it, just improve it. She was hearing what the staff was talking about around the hospital. It was losing revenue, and jobs were being lost. It would only be a matter of time before the doors would close on her. It was called downsizing. The evidence from sales was all down, so it would only be a matter of time. She found out she was not the only one with a pink slip at the end of the day. She was not surprised. The rumors that the doors of the hospital were going to close had been in the air for a while. She knew losing revenue without profit was only going to be a matter of time before everybody would be on the unemployment line. There was no consolation in the situation now. She could plan what her next move would be, and it had to be a master plan. Karen's thoughts were more than just about providing for herself; she also had Kenyuna to think about. Here they came rolling to the front of her mind in the still of the day, with the house clean and dinner on the stove.

She sat waiting for Kenyuna to walk in the door any minute now. She was old enough now, and she had come a long way. She had her own friends and her own after-school activities; she was busy. She had come into her own identity just a year ago. She was a smart, soon-to-be teenager with a different personality from Karen. She was very quiet and easygoing and only spoke when she had something to say. They were two different personalities. Karen loved to talk and express what was on her mind. Kenyuna held on to issues, problems, and concerns. Karen would have to pull them out of her. She knew the built-up anger and unhappiness she held inside could harm her later on in her life. She was glad she had taken classes in this area about coping with built-up stress. She could use her skills now to help Kenyuna cope with her issues.

Mr. Poole and Karen really worked well together, and he shared parts of his life with her. He lived with his girlfriend for the last several years; she had two children that were not his. He was the father figure in their life, and he shared the responsibility of helping raise them with their mother. He did not have any biological children of his own. Karen did not ask why, and he did not share with her the reason he did not have children. She saw the expression on his face that it was something that he did not want to talk about. His conversation did express that he was not that happy in the relationship and that he felt that his girlfriend had the upper hand on him because he paid most of the bills. They had an arrangement with her children since their biological fathers were not in the picture. They worked out some kind of arrangement. Since he had been raising them for some years now, they had worked it out so that they both got what they needed. Karen felt a little sorry for him, but not really. It's what men should do to take care of their families. He was the man of the house. He was doing what a man does for his household and family. She knew there are always two sides to every story, and that one side may not be the whole story. She didn't want the relationship to move any farther than it was. They would just be friends after hearing Mr. Poole's side.

She and Mr. Poole just stayed study partners and kept their GPA stable and assignments turned in on time. They made arrangements every week for study time, and if calls were needed, she always contacted him at work. If she missed a class, she would get the notes from him in their next shared class. He took great notes. It was a great partnership. The respect level stayed straight. Mr. Poole never got out of his lane with Karen, and she respected his lane. The semester went by really fast, and the year went even faster. She and Mr. Poole were comfortable with where they stood. They would buy lunch for each other, and most of the time, she was the one short on cash. She could ask him for a few bucks to get her through until a check from her part-time job came through. She could depend on Mr. Poole; he always seemed to have the money, whatever the amount she asked to borrow. Mr. Poole knew she was good for it when she told him she would pay him back. She always kept her promise to pay him back. It was her bond. If she shook hands on it, she did what she said she would.

She did not want to damage the trust and friendship she had developed with him, nor did she want to lead him on in any way. She felt that he wanted more from her than a typical college student relationship. She kept her distance, keeping it on a professional level. He would make remarks over breakfast or lunch study sessions, which was uncomfortable for her. She would often laugh it off or make a joke about what he had said to clear the air. He would back off and go back to the agenda. Even though they had become very close friends, she wanted to keep it that way. She knew all too well how it could turn out through trial and error. She knew she could have a friendship with a man without being in a sexual relationship with him. Especially when she was not attracted to him or wanted to be intimate with him.

He was a nice man and a good person, but whatever he was trying to get out of here, or whatever the case was, she was not going to be the one to bail him out of anything. He knew her situation as well as she did; a single woman was not an invitation for him. They did not hang out or meet after school; their schedules did not permit it. He did not see her with any guy friends that he knew of. He was far from being a stupid man. She had to be as smart, if not smarter than he was. She kept blocking all the angles that he came at her with. She just did not want any more headaches at the time. She kept him at a distance regarding her personal life from that point on. She would keep the

52

subject around him, his life, and how life was treating him as a man. She already had a front-row seat to life as a woman.

He was so comfortable with her that he shared the racism that he has to endure as a black man working in white corporate America. He was passed over for several promotions in Police Department positions he knew he was qualified for, only to be told he did not have a college degree for the position, which was a requirement to advance to those positions with better pay. This was the main reason he was in college, but once other white officers found out he was in college, they began harassing him for being in college. They would have extra work for him to do to keep him from studying when there was no booking for the night in the station. They told him that he could not study on the job, but the white staff would sit around and read the newspaper for hours. Some would be studying for a station exam and on-the-job advancement just like him. Mr. Poole felt the need to share his stories and his pain with her, and she could relate to him. She had also felt that same discrimination in her lifetime working in white corporate America. She knew his pain, and she gave him some advice that worked well in her situation. She felt it would work for him. His supervisor called him into his office and told him that he could not bring any books or study material to work with him while on duty. Mr. Poole told the supervisor that he hopes that will apply to everybody working the same shift with him. Mr. Poole asked him the difference between reading newspapers or magazines at the desk and reading a college book.

She did not see him after that for a few days. She was so anguished to find out how things were going for him at work. He told her that his supervisor never said anything else to him about reading at the desk. She was so happy for him that he stood up for himself. He did not take what was good for the goose and was not good for the geese. He and Karen finished their studies at the community college level and looked forward to continuing on to the university level.

Their relationship continued as it had been since the day they first met. The feeling was mutual. She felt he had her back, and she had his. She did not know if her GPA would be enough to get her into a university. She had failed some classes and was still trying to decide what her interest in studying was. She submitted her application anyway and waited for her letter of admission. Now she would take some time out and enjoy the rest of the summer.

She still worked her part-time job and showed up at Kenyuna's school unexpectedly at times. She rested and relaxed the rest of the time, preparing her mind and body for the next stage of college life. She made arrangements with the college adviser and counselors and waited for her to accept the letter so she could enroll for the fall semester. She called Mr. Poole so they could work as much as their schedules allowed together. He had already enrolled to take Criminal Justice. Karen chose studies in sociology and family studies. She knew that their journey had come to an end. She felt sadness in the pit of her stomach; she felt an emptiness. The one thing she would take away from this encounter, relationship, and friendship was the determination to continue the education she had promised herself long ago. And if you can't keep a promise to yourself, who can you keep a promise to?

Mr. K was not just a lover to her; he was an inspiration, just what she needed now and that only a man could do. He encouraged her to go for her Master's degree, letting her know she was smart enough to achieve anything she wanted to. She appreciated his support. She was just trying to get to the next step, which was the university level. He told her that anything hard was worth working for and that it would pay off in the end. She placed those words deep inside herself as the semester came to an end in the next few weeks. She didn't have any other contact with Mr. K, but he would never leave her heart or mind for a long time. There are very few people that cross your path who are truly interested in your well-being and encourage you to succeed or even want you to succeed. He was one of those guys who was just there to complete his internship for a few semesters before becoming a professor. He was a long way from home. She knew that feeling herself. She was attracted to him and felt the feeling was mutual. They did what was mutual, and one conversation turned into, "Can you come over and hang out and have some dinner?" She had this encounter before. It was just an instant connection; there was no attachment. She didn't want to be in his life, and he didn't want to be in hers after a few nights together as two consenting adults. She knew Mr. K was not there to stay. She had her work cut out for her already, and she didn't need any distractions. They did what two mature adults did for both of them at the time and kept it at that. Some months had passed when Mr. K called her to wish her the best in her studies and to encourage her to continue her education. She told him she hoped that all was well back in his hometown with his family and daughter.

He told her he had enjoyed his stay in the city and was glad that they had met. She wished him well and hoped that he would get the professor job he had applied for. She knew this was another part of her life that would impact her life forever, helping her to keep moving forward. She took a work–study position in the dean's office for the next few semesters. It would be her last semester on the college campus. She thought this would give her some extra money while earning her a few credit hours as an intern a few hours a day. So why not? She didn't have a real job to report to every day anyway. This office management job would give her skills she would need later and give her a good look at corporate America. Working with other kinds of people, she had not been in this environment for a long time. She worked in a one-person office for several years part-time. The only contact she had was with the men who came into the office once a week for a meeting. If someone came into the office for information, a question, or a payment, she enjoyed it. She knew that she would have to venture out into corporate America, so this was her opportunity to get started. The intern program would only be for the remaining semesters she had left, which was fine with her. She would only work a few hours in the morning, giving her enough time to get to her part-time job in the afternoon.

The dean's office was quiet and isolated, and very few people were permitted in. Everyone had to make appointments to see the chancellors. She did not see him very often herself. She was functioning as the secretary's assistant to the chancellor. She made arrangements for retreats, did receptionist work, made copies, prepared documentation for meetings, assisted with lunches and office staff breaks, faxed documentation—you name it, she did it. She learned all that she could about making an office function like one. She really did enjoy the opportunity presented by this office experience.

It was getting close to time to leave for the day. She was asked to drop some documents off at the office of another assistant manager. She walked into his office with the documents to sign and returned to the dean's office the next day. She sat waiting for him, and he began a conversation with her.

"So what is your major?"

"Sociology," she replied.

"That field of study does not pay very much money."

What he said made her angry. She sat even taller and prepared herself for a battle.

She replied with an even voice, her voice carrying a long distance.

"Well," she said, "it may not pay much money, but it's not always about the money; it's how happy you are with what you are doing in your life. I've not known anyone who had a lot of money and took it with them when they died. Word for thought."

Do money and possessions make any person good? She didn't think so.

He nodded his head. "Thank you. Have a good day."

"Likewise," she said as she walked out of his office.

She did not see him after that encounter for a while. She heard he took a position as a director at some community organization working with disadvantaged children. She thought to herself, Now go figure. A non-profit organization. I wonder how that is working out for Mister.

She never spoke about a person's career choice if it was important to them. She just didn't know what they would be doing in the future. It may not pay as much money as one might think it should, but sometimes the rewards outweigh the money. She kept her degree field and took a seminar class off campus when she saw Mister again. He did not recognize her, but she remembered him. She even had the opportunity to look at him up close and personal as he stood shaking hands with the guests who had come to hear him speak. She looked right into his face and smiled. He looked worn out and tired. She wondered if the money was worth it and how that was working out for him as the youth director. She was glad that she did not let his words discourage her from doing what she felt was right for her. Maybe he had encouraged her to continue on the path she was on. She could tell him what she was about to achieve and how hard it had been to get to where she was. Instead, she left with her head held high as she breathed in the fresh, cool air of the day. With the sunshine hitting just the right part of her neck, she headed toward the car. She had another busy day ahead of her tomorrow, with two classes waiting for her. She needed to focus on them as she pushed Mister to the back of her mind, never giving him another thought.

Karen was so glad that Kenyuna was in her last year of school. She did not have to worry about changing her school or moving to another school. The school district was in a mess, and parents were moving their children out of the district in large numbers. Other districts were putting requirements in place for children to attend their school districts. Things didn't get any better for the failing school districts that Kenyuna once attended, but she was glad that her child did not have to endure the mess that so many people had created. It seemed that no one had any concern about what was best for the thousands of children who already had several strikes against them: low-income families, African American children, and single parents with limited child support. She knew well the disadvantages these children faced. She lived in the same community. She had firsthand knowledge of their situations, and the news media did not have to inform her. She had her own eyewitness account of the failing school issues surrounding her. She and the rest of the African American people were never to be educated anyway, under slavery or even now. She was glad that Kenyuna was not going to be a part of that mess anymore. Teachers were losing their jobs, children were threatening teachers, children were bringing weapons to school, drugs were in school, and the dropout rate was through the roof. Children with ADHD and their parents made excuses on that basis for their children being out of control. Most parents were too busy working for minimum wage; they could barely put food on the table. She was struggling with one child. She could not imagine what it would be like with two children. The educated people were even the worst people to represent the rest of the uneducated people. Somehow, when your motive is recognition, power, and control, whatever you start out committed to doing will fall by the wayside. Some people were looking for validation from other people. That was what they longed for. What was best for all was for her not to live there anymore.

She was sad because it was true that she would do her part as a parent to help in any way she could. Even if she did not have her degree, she remembered all the wonderful teachers Kenyuna had along the way and what they had given toward her education to help her feel good about herself. The least she could do was stand with them when they needed support to fight the powers that be. The district was not making good decisions for the whole, and she felt compassion for them all, especially for the teachers she had gotten to know over the years.

BUTTERFLY SEVEN: THE LAST IS THE HARDEST

Karen had several assignments to complete, a few of which she knew she would have to work hard to get a high grade on. It did not help her chances that she did not like the professor in the class. She had spent extra time researching all the data for the assignment. She was sure she would get the grade she wanted. His grading scale was different from all the others she had had in the past. He graded on a much larger scale, making it difficult for even the smartest student to pass his class. She thought he was just a real butthead, but she was determined to beat him at his little tricks. She felt that he was just out to get everybody to prove that he was in charge. They had to dance to his tune, which she disliked. She hated it. She turned in her assignment as scheduled and knew that she had done a good job on it, still hoping she would at least get a B, if not a higher grade, on it. A few days passed, and everybody was on pins and needles waiting to get their last assignment back from Mr. Butthead. It was the last day of his class, and she could not wait to be away from him.

"Karen," he called. "Your paper."

She could not see the grade. It was on the last paper, and she flipped the pages fast to see before heading back to her desk. She was surprised when she noticed the C on her paper. She was shocked, so she waited until after class to confront him about the grade. She felt she did not deserve the grade; she had worked hard on this assignment. He would have to explain to her what was wrong with her paper and why she deserved a C.

Karen arranged the meeting with Mr. Butthead for the following week; she just had to get this concern out in the open once and for all. She had named him a few days into the class. She sat in his office, waiting for her turn to enter. She noticed one student after another exiting with their heads down. It was not a good sign for her. She built up her courage when she heard her name called.

"Have a seat," he told her without looking up from the paper in front of him. "What can I do for you?"

Mr. Butthead, she hoped that did not come out of her mouth. "I do not understand how I got a C on this assignment."

"Well, your paper was good," he informed her, "but my grading scale is a little different, which makes it hard for anyone to get a grade above a C in my class regardless of how smart they are or how well the assignment is written."

"Can I do some extra credit assignments to get a better grade before the end of the semester grades are recorded?"

"The grade is the grade," Mr. Butthead said.

She knew that was his final answer. What an arrogant butthead, she thought. She had no other choice but to dance to his music, and she was happy that she would never have to see him again. She would take her C grade and hope that it would not interfere with her admission to the university in the fall. She hoped that Mr. Butthead would be the last instructor she would encounter for a long time. She did not want or need to deal with a college instructor like him to finish her college goal. She would talk with Poole about this situation. It was always good to have another perspective on the situation. She had always found that two heads thinking together were always better than one. She and Poole would join forces with the classes they took together and end their last semester with great GPA scores. She learned that the C grade did not do too much damage to her GPA score. Not bad for a woman who had not been to college for some years—not bad at all, she thought to herself.

She had completed two years of college, and Kenyuna had graduated from high school. She had a part-time job and was currently admitted to a university to start in the fall. She even found time to teach in her church's Sunday School class in the mornings. Her self-esteem was as high as it could be. She felt like a new person in the same old skin. Her life was just where she wanted it to be. She was glad she stuck with it. She had arranged her schedule so well that she could work a part-time job during the evening and earn a little extra income. Kenyuna was now taking her college courses, playing basketball, and working a full-time job as well. Things were finally looking like they were on track. She could see a pretty good future ahead.

She got hired as a desk counselor for a Federal Release Program for inmates trying to reenter society after being paroled. She could see her studies paying off. It gave her the opportunity to assist women and men to stay on the right path to becoming good citizens in the community. The experience showed her that some people are going to do good or evil, and they have a choice to do one or the other. She learned that no one can change another person's behavior. The change had to come from the person who wanted to change their behavior. She learned a lot from the counselor position, being responsible for keeping track of all the clients and knowing their movements at all times. She had to make sure that the clients were not in places they were not supposed to be. They could not be in parts of the city where there were any illegal activities, often having to endure random drug and alcohol testing. She had visitations with each client weekly to update their parole status, which kept them on parole. It was part of the federal parole law they had to comply with while on parole. She saw all kinds of people on parole, from the high class to the middle class and to the low class, from the poor to the wealthy. She enjoyed the job and the learning experience of dealing with people that society had written off as a menace to society. She felt right in this position, and she did all she could to assist them in achieving their goal, not wanting any of them to return to prison for parole violations.

She would have liked it if all the clients she assisted wanted to become the best they could be.

She was realistic and knew that some people just will not, cannot, and do not want to do right. It is what it is. She thought about how easily one of the women in this place could have been her, and how easily she could have made just one wrong decision and been walking in their shoes. She thought how blessed she had been not to have taken the same road. She sat listening to story after story from the clients about how hard it had been to be incarcerated and separated from family and how it had changed their lives forever. The clients ranged from mothers, fathers, and grandparents to businesspeople, dentists, judges, city councilmen, sisters of sisters, and brothers of brothers. Some had spent years incarcerated after making that one wrong decision that took them away from their families for a long time. She left that job each day grateful and even more appreciative of the life she had with Kenyuna.

Her clients had a lot of baggage attached to them. She was part of the world they were mad at. She endured the hard work and the verbal abuse that came with the job; some days were better than others. She often reminded her clients of the situation they were in because of the choices they had made. They did not want to do anything that would incarcerate them again. Most of the time, the reminder worked to their advantage. She didn't need to call for assistance that day. It also put her at ease working the job, knowing that the police department was just across the street with several large policemen working the same shift and a panic button so close that she could push it anytime she needed it. She felt the toll of working part-time while being a full-time college student and juggling keeping a roof over her head and Kenyuna's. It was catching up with her. She was feeling the wear and tear on her physical and mental health. She knew she would not last much longer on this schedule. She found herself doing homework at home and at work, and she had to do an assignment for a class every week. They were coming faster than she could keep up. She found the strength and power within herself to keep up without dropping a class that semester. She was determined that she would not fail college this time around. If she didn't do something, all her hard work would be in vain. She gave her employer her notice of resignation, although the extra income was pretty helpful. The price of staying for the money was just too high for her. Kenyuna was doing well in school, so they could spend a little more time together, something she had not been able to do with her in a while because of her demanding schedule.

Karen could really see the fruits of her labor in Kenyuna. She was a beautiful young lady, and she felt she had done a pretty good job raising her all by herself. Although Kenyuna had given her some sleepless nights, causing her one or two situations that she had to work hard to get out of. She could not see anything that growing pains had caused or anything she had done to change her love for her. When it was almost time for Kenyuna to graduate from the two-year college, Karen had to make a decision. She could advise her to stay in the state and attend one of the many universities in the community or let her make up her own mind.

She wanted her to make an adult decision for her future. She was given a scholarship to attend college a few hours or farther away. It was the decision she would let her make. Karen had to let her go to become the person she should be. Karen had learned that when things are going well, it is always the calm before the storm, and the storm did come. She felt she had done her best to get her to the young adult stage. Now it was time to let her go, even if she knew her age did not make her an adult. She wanted a car, and Karen was reluctant, although Kenyuna had been driving a car for a while. She was responsible. Karen was still not sure that she was ready for her own car with all the responsibility that came along with it. Kenyuna had worked hard and saved her money for the down payment. She promised Karen that she would not have to help her with that. She did have a full basketball scholarship she had received from Lincoln University, which was two or three hours away. Karen was having difficulty processing all this. She just did not want her little girl far away from her. She had always looked out for both of them, making sure they were safe and secure. Time went on, and she and Kenyuna talked. She was still uncomfortable with the idea. The fact was that she could not be with Kenyuna forever. She knew she had to let her go. Maybe it would be better for both of them if it happened sooner rather than later. They both prepared themselves emotionally for the changes that they both knew they would be going through soon.

Kenyuna received her admission documents from the university to start the fall semester of that year. It made the summer go by so fast for her. Kenyuna was excited and started stocking items she would need for her on-campus lifestyle.

Karen tried hard to prepare herself for when she would miss not being home with her every day. It was time to look for a car. She knew her sister was good at finding a good car for a reasonable amount of money. Karen drained her little savings account to make her daughter happy. She was so proud of what she had accomplished. Kenyuna promised that she would be a responsible young adult, so she gave her the benefit of the doubt. She went ahead and co-signed for the car, even though deep within her soul, she did not feel right about doing it. Kenyuna had done well, and she had convinced her that she would pay the car off in a few months from her work and financial aid. That sounded good to Karen. It was what helped her put pen to paper.

When the storm comes, it's bad. She was the co-signer for that car her daughter wanted so badly. Kenyuna left for college with all her belongings in her new car. It was a joyful day for her. Karen had an empty feeling; her nerves were jumping out of her body. The time had come for Kenyuna to go, and Karen helped her put her items in the car. They spent the last two weeks talking and hanging out together. Karen was still so sad inside that she tried to share the pitfalls of campus living with her daughter. Although she had never lived on a college campus, the information she had came from talking with college peers and their parents. She would watch programs on television about things that happen to young people on college campuses. What she heard and saw was not that good; some of it was downright bad. Karen knew that since she had raised Kenyuna well, she would have to believe Kenyuna would make the right decisions. She knew she had shown and talked a lot, hoping she had taught her about the dangers that were out there in the world she was sending her into to live her life. They both lay in her bed, the two of them watching the news together about the good, bad, and ugly in the world. Karen tried to explain the bad things people would do to one another if they had the opportunity. She shared that some people pretend to be good, but deep down they are very evil people who live among us all. It was all she could give her daughter: the tools to be aware of her surroundings and to be very cautious with those whom she considered friends.

Karen felt well. It looked like things would work out alright. She settled down and got used to being alone, doing some of the things she wanted to do without having to get home at a certain time or worry about cooking dinner. She checked her next day's assignments, talked with a few people on the phone, and thought she had herself to be with. She felt she had worked hard enough to get to this time and place in her life. She would reap the benefits, and it felt good.

Something caught her attention. It was several weekends before she noticed Kenyuna was coming home every other weekend. That was just too often for her. Karen did not question her about coming home. She did miss her, but not every other weekend. She had made an arrangement with the car company to contact her if Kenyuna did not make her car payment. She made an arrangement with the college to contact her if Kenyuna did not keep her grade up. She knew that Kenyuna's stay on campus was based on the regulations and guidelines of a signed contract agreement. She had to keep a good GPA to continue getting free accommodations. So far, so good—she had completed her first, second, and third semesters with flying colors. Karen was happy that her daughter was smart. It was proven by the good report she received from the college. She did not let Kenyuna know that she was getting reports per semester; she did not feel she needed to tell her. It all fell apart. Karen opened her mail to find a notice for two months' worth of unpaid car payments. Karen called Kenyuna immediately, but she got no answer in her dorm room. She left a message.

"Ms. Kenyuna, when you get this message, you need to call your mother ASAP."

She had a bad feeling about this situation. If she was not paying the car payments, what else was she not doing or telling her? The child had lost her mind. She had failed all her classes in the second semester. Karen was on the warpath; she had to find out what was going on, and she needed to find out soon. She called the college office early the next day to speak with Kenyuna's coach; he was not available. She had met him, and he had assured her that if there was anything she needed regarding Kenyuna, she should feel free to contact him.

He had told all the parents that his basketball girl would be too busy to get into trouble. He would keep an eye on all his girls with his assistant coach. He thanked all the parents for letting him have our daughters for the next two years. Now she felt all that talk was hogwash, or, in short, bull. She left messages for Mr. Coach, waiting for a return call from him immediately, or she would be taking a trip to that university. The call came right on time, and the wait was well worth it. She was not prepared for what Mr. Coach had to say to her. She was just not ready. She had to sit down. The conversation took hours. Mr. Coach explained all that was going on with her daughter. Kenyuna was not going to basketball practice, she was not paying her car payments, and she had gotten caught shoplifting. She was partying all night and sleeping all day, not attending any classes. He said she had not been to the last three basketball practices, and he had been trying to get in touch with her. Karen was furious as he told her that Kenyuna had forced him to drop her from the team. Her blood pressure shot through the roof, and her head started to spin out of control.

"Thank you, Mr. Coach."

She did not even want to go to work the next day. She had not slept at all. She thanked God that she did not have class. She decided not to even go to work because she had too much to deal with. She called the loan officer about the car to see if anything could be worked out regarding the missing car payments. In the meantime, she still had not heard from Kenyuna. She had to know by now that her dirty little secrets were out. Karen left several messages for her. She figured she needed time to get her thoughts together.

"Mom, hello."

"Kenyuna, what the hell is going on? You are failing out of college and getting kicked off the basketball team. You promised you would pay for that car, which I spent some of my money on too. Now, what are you going to do?

I will tell you what. Since you refused to do a damn thing in college, pack your shit up and get your ass out here. You can get a job and help pay some of these living bills here."

There was silence on her end of the phone as Karen talked. That was her final answer. She knew what her daughter had been doing at college for the last year, and she did not want to hear anything else. She could not think straight; she had to figure out how she was going to get herself out of this mess. The car company was now calling her for past payments she missed so she could catch them up. She thought about her first instinct. It was right on point. She had made a big mistake. Never ever would she co-sign for anything else with anybody, nor would she ask anybody to co-sign for her. That car drained her account. She was glad that she had put some money away for hard times.

She made Kenyuna work hard until she paid every penny back to her. She learned her lesson. She remembered what her good old grandmother had told her when she was young. Big Mom would often say, "Bought sense is better than no sense at all." I'm sure everyone has a "Big Mom" sounding off in their ear when they do something stupid or wrong.

Within the next few months, Karen put her foot down hard. Kenyuna could only do or say as much as she would allow her to do and say—even less. That was just enough while she lived under her roof. Kenyuna had decided that she would like to go to a trade school to get a certificate in the medical field. Karen thought that was a good thing for her to do. She was getting tired of working long hours in the fast food industry. It was not paying her the kind of money she wanted to get where she wanted to go. With the payments to pay off the car, kicking in on the bills, and an outing with her friend, the money was just not going far enough for her to get ahead. Karen felt her growing pains, and she did not lift a hand to assist her at all. She let her handle it the way Kenyuna's grown butt wanted to. She enrolled as a medical code and billing specialist. She could complete the course in nine to twelve months. Karen knew she could complete the course with her eyes closed; at the same time, she could do a little guiding and keep an eye on her. She had rules. If you did not go to school or to the army, then everybody in the house got a job and paid bills. She was glad she did not have a car. She did not like it or have time to take her to school and work every day. Karen worked every day to get herself to the places she needed to be. She was just not going to become the house taxi for Kenyuna.

She had as many places to be as she did, and it was not going to work out well. The evening was TGIF. Karen wanted to just hang out, have a drink, and relax before heading home. Today she would be the taxi and pick Kenyuna up on the way home. You just can't prepare yourself for things out of the blue while on the way home.

Kenyuna said she wanted to become a bartender. It was fast money; the course would only take a short length of time. After six to eight weeks, she said she would be a bartender. Karen had always encouraged her daughter that if she put her mind to anything with hard work, she could do it. Kenyuna did just that. She started her course to become a bartender. Karen let her little girl grow into the woman she wanted to be by setting an example for her to follow. She had only a few more semesters at the trade college before completing her studies. Karen would be done with college. She had enough of school. She was tired. The sacrifice was a great one; she had settled for part-time wages to get by. It was time for her hard work to pay off. She had done it her way, making sure that life would finally deal her and Kenyuna a hand of all A's.

Months had passed, and things were as good as they could be as she and Kenyuna sat and watched TV. It was a quiet night; neither of them had much to do. She had a little studying to do. It felt good not to worry about reading or writing an assignment for another class. BOOM. And then it happened.

"Mom, can I ask you something?"

"What is it, Kenyuna?"

"I would like to find another car."

Karen could have just fallen right off the couch. She just sat there for a few moments. The nerve of this child, she thought.

The one she brought into this world had the nerve to ask her to assist her with purchasing another car for real. "Oh, my goodness!"

After all the hell they had been through with the other car, she said, "NO!" She was done for the night and headed toward her bedroom. Her child must be crazy, or something is wrong with her. She didn't care what she did to get that car. It was a done deal as far as she was concerned. She caught the bus until she had enough money to purchase whatever car she wanted. Not one dime would be coming from her pocket or her resources to help with another car for the rest of her life.

"Mom, I'm a more mature person now that I've made a big mistake, and everybody makes mistakes, even you, mom."

"Well-spoken, my daughter, but you're still not getting a dime."

Karen held to her decision. She had to give her daughter some brownie points for that one. God knows that she made mistake after mistake. She accepted her mistakes a long time ago and will make some more. She put them to rest today. It would be years before she made this mistake again. With that said, it was the end of that conversation about a car. Kenyuna never talked to her about it again. They would drive the car they had and take care of it for many years, and they would learn to appreciate it at the same time.

Karen felt that the mother-and-daughter relationship had ended that night. She knew she would no longer treat her as her little girl but as Kenyuna, the young adult woman she had become. She could finally see the light at the end of the tunnel. She sat quietly, doing nothing. She took a look back at the hard times she had endured getting through college, raising a child alone, spending long nights studying, and worrying about Kenyuna. She also kept a roof over their heads to find whatever finances were needed to do it all. She was pretty proud of herself for the way she had handled it all without having to turn into someone or do something she had seen other ladies do to survive. She knew that things were going to be good soon, so she braced herself. There was always something looming in the shadow that the eyes could not see or the ears had not heard. Her instinct was her saving grace.

A knock on the door brought her back into the real world. She wondered who in the world that could be. She knew that Kenyuna was out with friends and probably would not be coming back until late. It was the parents of the young lady who lived below them. Kenyuna and their daughter had taken a man's car that had been over at their house at a party. Once the party was over, it was time for everybody to go home. No one at the party knew where Kenyuna and the young lady were. They had left in the man's car. It finally dawned on the parents that they had the man's car. The parents said they had already checked places they might have gone in the car and there was nothing else they could do. They just wanted her to know what was going on, and they were sorry about the situation. Karen stayed up all night watching and waiting, hoping and praying that they would return okay. She finally fell asleep on the couch as the sun was rising in the window and shining brightly into her face. She pulled herself from the couch and toward Kenyuna's room to find her sound asleep in bed.

"Kenyuna, what happened last night? Your friend's parents were here and said you and her had stolen a man's car."

"Don't worry about it, Mom. It was no big deal."

"What do you mean it's not a big deal?"

"He gave us the keys to the car. We did not take anything from anybody."

"Girl, what if you had damaged that man's car? You would be in a world of trouble."

That sounded like my mother, she thought.

She rolled over and went back to sleep. Karen did not hear a word for weeks about the man's car. She found out later that the man's car had been damaged and left on a street in the city. She assumed the man was embarrassed or just counted it as a loss. He did not report the car as stolen. Kenyuna was so close to paying off her car debt. Karen just wanted to be done with it; the sooner the better for both of them. Karen just needed a shoulder to vent on, so she called her dear friend Poole.

"Hi."

"Girl, what's going on?" he said. He knew it was unusual for her to call him; it had to be important.

"What's up, Poole?"

"I just wanted to tell you that you were right." He had told her not to purchase that car for Kenyuna because she was too young. She wished she would have listened to him.

"She lost the car. I'm not going to spend another dime helping her get another one. I have done all I'm going to do for that child. She has made her bed, and she is going to lie in this one. I'm going to have to bite the bullet on my credit report. It brought this lesson better late than never."

"Yeah, I hear you, girl. You know they will be coming for you."

"Ah, I know. I'm trying to settle with them now; I can't get much from a turnip now."

"Okay, I've got to go. I'll see you at school this week."

"Bye."

He was right; he had told her not to do it because, even though Kenyuna seemed mature and responsible, she wasn't. His words would haunt her. She knew now that she should have listened to Poole in the first place. That decision was still biting her in the butt long after it had been settled and done with. Karen's parenting skills had started really kicking in, and there was no book to teach her how to deal with young adult children. She was doing the things that moved you from childhood to adulthood. Karen could relate to that. She had to go through that same phase. It was a process, not a drama. She remembered how it was with her mother. She recalled the snappy remarks, the lack of response to questions, the leaving without telling her mother, the not coming home at night, and the not calling to let her know she was alright.

The day her mother lost it, she didn't remember what she did to set her off. She ended up running from the house to her grandmother's house. Her mother had knocked her down on the floor and was on top of her, slapping her face. She got away from her without knowing how she did it. She ran out the kitchen door and down the street to her grandmother's house.

Her grandmother could see something had happened, but she did not ask any questions. She just said, "You can stay here tonight. You'll go back home tomorrow and apologize to your mother for your behavior."

Karen was so thankful for her grandmother's understanding that she just sat there on the porch with her for the rest of the day. She did not want to go anywhere. She learned that day that she needed to respect her mother, even if she felt she was all grown up.

She was really at her wit's end with Kenyuna. She had made some not-so-good choices so far. She was not pleased with any of them. Kenyuna had a car repossessed; she dropped out of college; and she was hanging out with the kind of people she did not approve of. Karen had learned over her lifetime that not everyone is a good friend. Friends are not there to bring you down, but to lift you up. She could see her daughter hanging out with some of the wrong kinds of friends that just did not fit the lifestyle she had hoped for her.

The close bond was broken when the police came knocking at the door. She was looking over her class schedule for a test she had early the next morning. She had done all the studying she needed to get an A on the test. She thought she would just look over her notice one last time before she called it a night when she heard a knock on the door. She headed toward the door, wondering who that could be. She was not expecting any company tonight.

"Is Kenyuna your daughter?" the cop asked.

"Yes," Karen replied.

"Is she here?"

"No, what is the problem, officer?"

"We believe that she may have stolen some property from an office building she was hired to clean by a cleaning company."

"What property are you talking about, officer?"

"There were a few computers and personal property from the staff office desk stolen."

Karen knew that Kenyuna had started working for a cleaning company during the evening. She could not believe that she would get caught stealing. She remembered when she was about Kenyuna's age, how she had made the same mistake—shoplifting—and what it almost cost her. She hoped that Kenyuna was not headed in that direction and would put her foot down, or she would put it in her butt. She had not worked this hard to see Kenyuna heading in that direction. It had been a long journey. This would haunt her for the rest of her life if she did nothing to intervene. Kenyuna was far from a bad person or even disrespectful toward her. Karen knew that she had not given much thought to the consequences of stealing as an adult from the law's perspective. She knew Kenyuna didn't have a clue; she was still not mature enough to handle the responsibility for her actions as an adult. She was now playing in the grown-up, real adult world. Even though she had not been in that world for a long time, Karen knew from her experiences that it was not good.

She asked Kenyuna if she could talk with her as soon as possible. It was very important to talk. The day had been long and hard. She was tired and trying hard to keep her mind on the test. But the conversation she needed to have with Kenyuna today kept running into her thoughts. She managed to push the thought of anger to the side for now in order to complete the task at hand, which was to pass this final class. She would go by the office to check any emergency mail that needed her attention today.

It would give her some quiet time to calm down and think about exactly what she wanted to discuss with her daughter. She had a final look over her study notes before the next test in the afternoon. She grabbed her book bag and headed toward the door. She looked around for one last check before closing the door behind her.

She had asked Kenyuna to be home no later than six o'clock. She thought they could have a light dinner and a lot of conversation. She picked at her food, even though she was hungry. She would break the silence.

"How was your day?"

"Fine mom," Kenyuna said.

"Kenyuna, I love you. I do not want you to get into any trouble with the police. If you cannot do what I know is best for you, I know what you have been doing. I have no other choice but to tell you like it is. You are no longer a child. You will go to jail for whatever you do from this point on as far as breaking the law. I will not spend my hard-earned money getting you out of jail. You have two choices: one is going back to college and getting a degree, or getting a full-time job and paying half of the bills. I will not take care of a well-bodied person with good health who is smart and can achieve anything they put their mind to, just for you to do nothing in life."

Karen had to treat her like the adult she wanted to be. It was time for her to stand on her own two feet. Today was a good day to get her started. She knew that for her to get through this parenting experience, she would have to stick to her words and display some tough love, even if it hurt her more than it hurt Kenyuna. It was tough going, but once Kenyuna saw that Karen was not to be played with, she soon got the picture that the good times were over and all the extra financial benefits had ended. She soon realized that she could no longer get any extra anything. If she was out of gas and had no money until payday, she couldn't borrow a dime from mom. Bad behaviors do not get a good reward from mom or in society.

Kenyuna learned valuable lessons over the summer. She had lost her friends. When you are down and out, you see who your friends are. They seem to disappear when the good times are gone and when the ends are gone too.

Karen hoped her child would soon find out who her real friends are. She would figure that out on her own. Karen could not teach her that. She would be the one to pick her friends. She hoped she would pick one or two good ones. Karen was taking inventory. Kenyuna was not going out as much as she used to, and she was spending a lot more time in her room. Karen picked up an application from different places for full-time employment. Kenyuna had asked her to do that for her. Now progress was something she did not mind doing for her daughter as long as she could see her moving. She understood and felt the tightness in the air between the two of them, but she did not give a damn. She knew that Kenyuna was upset with her about the way she was treating her with limited attention. Karen walked in the door and just wanted to rest for an hour before dinner, maybe get a shower to clean up the dirt of the day before getting started. Kenyuna entered the kitchen and sat at the table with a smile on her face.

"Hi, Sweetie. How was your day?"

"I got the job, Mom, at Quick-Stop. They want me to come in tomorrow to finish filling out some paperwork. Can you drop me off in the morning at nine o'clock on your way to work?"

"That's great, Kenyuna; I can do that."

Karen was glad that she did not have a regular working schedule like most people. She had the flexibility that allowed her to do what she needed to during the day. She did not have any more early morning classes. Her morning was clear to do pretty much whatever. She wanted this child to get on with her life. The sooner she got money for gas or whatever she needed, the sooner she could take herself to work. Karen was determined not to give her a dime. She got herself into this situation, and she would work herself out of it. She can't get far without gas, she thought to herself. She prayed that Kenyuna would get the job. It would be the self-esteem boost she needed to get her back on track.

Kenyuna wanted to work full-time. She had made it perfectly clear that she was tired of going to school and that she needed a break from that world. Karen knew what her child was saying. She had been in school ever since she was two and a half years old. She was now a young adult. That was a lot of years of schooling, and Karen felt what she was saying. She was burned out from school and had lost total interest in it. Karen let her make that decision. She would help her stick with it, and maybe she would lighten up on her just a little bit. Karen knew college was a challenge. It was downright hard work. She understood that students, classes, and professors were all discipline things, especially when the professors were not nice. Some were mean as hell. It even took all her willpower not to drop out herself at some point. At times, the only thing that kept her on track and determined to finish was her little girl.

Kenyuna was working a regular weekly shift and getting paid weekly. The company needed someone to work overtime or stay late often. Kenyuna would often stay. She enjoyed this new job, and better yet, she liked the money even more. They worked out a schedule that did not interfere with Karen's schedule. Some nights, Karen did not want to get out of her warm bed to go get Kenyuna at midnight, especially when the weather began to turn cold and snowy. She figured that within a few months, Kenyuna would have enough money saved that she would be able to purchase a new car—something she could afford that was reliable—and that she would be paying for herself. She had learned her valuable lesson: she was not going down that road again.

Kenyuna had completed the medical course classes, which took several months to complete. Karen knew she could do it. She had applied right before getting the new job; she had to work it out. Karen was so proud of her for finally getting her life back on track. Karen knew she could. She was working a new job that she really liked. Karen thought to herself and smiled because she always knew that Kenyuna had it in her to do the right thing; she just needed her mom to guide her in the right direction. Karen knew she would now have a different relationship with her from that day forward.

It would change from her relationship with her little girl to a woman-to-woman relationship. Karen knew the decision she had made was the right one for her daughter to succeed. She thought a little tough love could go a long way after all. This had been one of the hardest things she had to do. She knew it was time to let her little girl go into the big world to make her own decisions. She told herself she would just be there for her whenever she needed her to be. Karen felt she had stood alone for so long that she once again had to make the tough decisions, arrangements, and plans for herself and Kenyuna. She was once again in a place that made her uncomfortable. She adjusted her thoughts and relaxed. Maybe this will be a part of her reality in this life for a long time to come. She was educated, financially stable, and independent—a woman who spoke her mind and made hard decisions that didn't make her popular. She thought about how, if she had never left Kenyuna's father, he would really come in handy right about now. Kenyuna would have listened to him more and paid more attention to him when he talked with her. She needed him during those tough days. What if the thought soon went away? She had made it this far, and she told herself she could finish this race without him. He did not send any child support, so why did she think he would give any emotional support to her now? Kenyuna was a young woman, and with each year of her getting to adulthood, Karen found them the most challenging years she had to face of all the years before. She settled into thinking as a single parent and continued to make the decisions and plans she would enjoy. Kenyuna could come along for the ride. She did not want to become selfish.

She told herself to be so independent that this life would take the place of having a meaningful relationship with the opposite sex. She would stick to the course she had promised herself and complete her college degree. Every day, life handed her a situation that she did not know what to do with, but she worked it out somehow. She worked it until it worked itself out. She was able to occasionally get a date here and there with some guys she met out and about, but nobody really made her feel like she was going to be an important person in their life other than God. Those relationships just fell by the wayside. Nothing was planted to make them grow. She just accepted that it is what it is. She did not waste her time with them once she found they were just a waste of her time. She found that most of them did not have any goals or future plans for their lives; they just lived from day to day. Some were even looking for a place to lay their heads at someone else's expense. She had learned by now that she could not raise another child because she did not want to. She was having a hard enough time raising her child into a woman. She already knew that was not going to happen. She had just never been in the cohabitation stage or the common-law marriage thing. She always remembered what her sweet old grandmother told her as a teenage child: "If a man can get the milk for free, then why would he purchase the cow?"

She did not find out how true that statement was until she met Rich. He came along like the wind. You know you can feel it; you can see it blow through the trees, and you can feel it on your skin. But you don't have a clue where it comes from or where it's going, what part of the earth it starts from, or how far it will go. That was the only way she could describe Rich. He was just there. He did not have anything special about him. His conversations stimulated her brain and kept her mind from thinking about all the things that were going on in her life at the time. His conversations were about church social events, their daily lives, or what her future plans were after finishing college.

She knew he was married, and that was a big turn-off for her. She just did not have any interest in any married men. She had heard about married men cheating on their wives from their family members, friends, and conversations with other women she knew. She did not want to get caught up in that kind of situation. Rich did not seem to be the type who even knew how to cheat on his wife; he was the straitlaced type of guy who made her feel safe with him. She did not worry about him stepping out of his comfort zone, and keeping him at bay seemed easy to do. As time passed, they got more comfortable with each other. He came around more often than a married man should. Their friendship turned into something more as he called more and more and began to fit right in. Rich kept asking her out to dinner, a movie, or to come over later; she knew she should have said "no." She thought it had been a while since she had been out on a date with any man, married or unmarried. It turned out not to be that bad. Rich was a real gentleman. He did not try anything. He pulled up in front of her apartment. She opened the car door to get out when he handed her an envelope.

"What is this?" she asked him.

He just smiled and said, "Good night."

She knew it was money, but she had no idea what it was for. Did she say something about finance being a little tight, or did they talk about money issues that she could not remember over the many conversations they had over the last few months? From that first outing with him, he often gave her money. She just could not understand why he did not seek any affection from her—no kissing, hand-holding, or touching. She found that strange but did not question his motives. She could use the extra cash for some bills or even a new pair of shoes. She noticed that Rich was stopping by her place more and more, which made her curious about what was really going on in his life.

Weeks turned into months before the relationship hit solid ground. She was deeper than she wanted to think. She had gone too far and lost the better part of her mind. He was a married man who had been in a committed marriage for some years.

She had been married. She knew how it felt, and she knew the pain she felt when it all came crashing down around her. She knew it would not last. She would have to do something about it now rather than later. Karen was preparing dinner when the phone rang. A soft voice spoke into the phone.

"Hello," the voice said, "are you messing around with my husband?"

She stood there. A few seconds had passed before she could even speak.

"You need to talk with your husband," Karen said.

"You know that he is a married man."

"Yes, he's your husband, not mine. Talk with him."

She put the receiver down as she stood there thinking about what just happened and how Rich's wife got her number. She felt embarrassed and ashamed that she had let this situation come right to her front door when she knew it would.

BUTTERFLY EIGHT: MARRIED/OUCH

Karen was not looking for this type of relationship. She really did not know how she had gotten herself into this mess. She had met Rick while working for a community outreach program after finishing her final internship to complete college. The final grade required some kind of community service to get her degree. It gave her a better outlook on job resources in the community. She would be the first candidate to apply for that position. It was a good opportunity to learn what the community had to offer her in her field of study. She just did not bother with the child support or family services programs.

Kenyuna's father was a deadbeat dad, which she had learned over the years. He and the new woman in his life had two or three children by now, and they were not doing well. He was still not working, living with his mother, and still using drugs. Kenyuna did not talk with him on a regular basis, but she kept in communication with her grandmother, her father's mother. She loved her father regardless of whether he was a part of her daily life. One thing about children and their distant parents is that they love them. Distance doesn't change that. Even if they are the worst parents on the planet and do nothing for them in life, that love will never change. Karen loved her child with an unconditional love that just couldn't be explained. She did not come between that father-daughter relationship she had with him. She knew that one day her daughter would find out just who her father was, and until then, she would not tell her. She let her love him even when he could not love her back in the way a father should. Karen felt she did not need to add to her daughter's heartache by bad-mouthing or degrading him. She had enough discussion inside of her about him for the both of them. She chose to keep them to herself. Kenyuna had enough to live with regarding her absent father, who abandoned her when she needed him the most. Karen did not want to push her child's mental stage over the edge by talking negatively about the only father she loved in her life. This conversation was taboo.

Kenyuna spent very little time speaking about her father. She just did not talk about him. When he did call, he knew where to find her. She often did not share their conversations with Karen. She would have to sort through it on her own so that it made perfect sense to her. One day she would be able to stop beating herself up with the "why me?" questions and get on with her life. Karen concluded that their relationship was best for her because of how they handled it. She did not care if Kenyuna spoke with her father or not. They would talk about him if she wanted to someday. Whenever he spoke to Kenyuna, he often left her with a message for Karen, telling her, "I still love her."

Karen would just smile and say okay in response to her daughter telling her what he had said. It showed her daughter that even though her father and mother were not together, she loved her by showing kindness. She could not give a damn if she ever saw him or spoke to him again, but she kept that to herself. Karen felt sad and hurt inside. She did not dare let her daughter see any of that on her face. Karen was disappointed in him, and Kenyuna was sad that he was not in her life as he should be. She knew the love she once had for him ran as long as the ocean and as wide as the sea. She would not damage the love Kenyuna had for her father. Their relationship was between them.

It was late, and she had a lot of things to do before going to bed. She was about to get started when the doorbell rang. She wondered who it could be. To her surprise, it was Rich standing at the door, wanting to come in. She really did not want to let him in. She could tell that something was bothering him by the way he was ringing the doorbell. She opened the door, and he came in. He told her that he just needed to talk with someone he considered a friend. Karen was glad she had completed most of the things she needed to do for the night. It turned out to be a long night for them. He ended up staying the night, sleeping on her sofa. She turned the light off and went to bed. He never got to the bottom of what was bothering him or what was going on with him. She was just too tired and sleepy to continue talking with him when she noticed he had fallen fast asleep on her couch.

By morning, he was gone. The cover was neatly folded at the end of the couch. He had left, and she did not have a clue what time he left; he was gone. She did not hear from him for a few days, which did not surprise her. She knew that he was a married man and that he could not pick up the phone and call her regularly. As a matter of fact, she was glad this was not going to work out anyway; she just did not want to be messing around with this man. It never turned out well for all parties involved. She never had any desire for or interest in several types of men; she kept to her high standards.

1. Don't do married men.

2. Don't do men with too many children. Three is too many for her.

3. Don't do old men.

4. Heterosexuals only.

Karen had a don't-do list that turned her off about some men, and she was wondering what happened to it pertaining to Rich. She just could not put her finger on what was wrong with him. He was not that attractive, she thought. He was a nice guy who owned his own business and drove a nice car—nothing fancy. He kept his hair clean and well-cut, was kind and easy to talk with, and always smelled really good. Nothing really turned her on when he walked into a room. Karen thought about what they had in common as she sat thinking about how nice he was. They had very few things in common—only a few things they shared: they both had one child, and they both enjoyed going to church. That was all she could come up with that they had in common. Maybe that was all that was needed to draw her to him and him to her—to make her like him. He had talent with words; he could have been a preacher or a great speaker if he wanted to. He had the skills to persuade you genuinely. She shared in conversation that she would be short on money until her next payday. He asked her how much she would need to hold her over. She said that a few hundred dollars would help her out a lot. She didn't expect him to do anything about it. Everybody has their own household to take care of. He had a wife. She knew the game. She had learned that most married men wanted the benefits without the responsibility.

The next morning, inside the drop mailbox, she found an envelope that had been left during the night. He had left an envelope in her drop box, and she knew it had to have been him. He did it after he was done with his cleaning service's night shift and on his way home. He called her the next day, asking her if she got it. He said it was late and he did not want to wake her, which seemed strange to her. Somehow it was so natural for him that she let him know they would talk later. She would let Rich know she appreciated what he did when they spoke again. She would pay him back the money. She had to do that because she was not trying to stay connected to him any longer. It was not feeling good. She could feel that in her soul.

Kenyuna was doing very well. She was happy with her job, and things were looking pretty good for her. She had not been in any trouble. Karen was still the taxi cab driver, even though that did not seem to bother her right now—she had always been a night owl anyway. So going to get Kenyuna from work at ten o'clock and sometimes having to wait for her had become part of the routine of her nightly schedule. It worked out fine for both of them, especially her; she did not have to make up any excuses for not seeing Rich. She often left Kenyuna asleep in the morning when she left for work. The daily routine often made them both too tired for conversation during the week. She did not feel anything out of sorts or pressing that she needed to share with Kenyuna; they just kept the routine as it was. The weekend was downtime for the both of them, and they often shared with each other over a good breakfast how the week before had gone. Sometimes there was only limited conversation between the two of them when their daily jobs involved having conversations with other people.

"Hi Rich, I have that money for you. When will be a good time for you to come by and get it?"

"Don't worry about it. Just keep it. I know how hard it is on single mothers. Buy your daughter something with it."

"No, I want to give it back to you."

"Okay, I'll get it from you later then."

"Okay."

Karen left the conversation without thinking about it again, and he never asked her for the money again. You just never know what you will get in a box of chocolate.

A few weeks went by, and Rich came by to talk. He told her he was a businessman. Businessmen knew lots of people, but she did not understand what he was talking about at the time. She just thought he was sharing information with her about his business to let her know. He was parked at her apartment when she pulled up, much to her surprise. He got out of his car as she got out of hers. His trunk had a lot of women's clothes inside. On this day, she was unsure what to think or do when she saw his vehicle full of women's clothes. He assured her that none of the clothes had been stolen and that he just wanted to do something nice for her. He told her the clothes were from business contacts he knew from his cleaning business. He told her to pick out whatever she wanted. They were really nice clothes, brand new, and some still had tags on them. Her mind flashed back to when he had asked her what size she wore, but she just did not answer him. She was reluctant to tell him at first because he was getting too personal for her. He began being persistent, so she told him. All the sizes she looked at were her size, and she could wear just about all of them. He even told her to pick out a few outfits she thought Kenyuna would like.

Karen had to know where he got all these clothes. He said he cleaned a department store building, and he and the owner were close friends. The clothes did not sell, so he sold them to his friends at a huge discount or let him take what he wanted as part of their contract to make room for the new arrival of clothes. Rich knew how to bait the fish and pull it in, and she was the fish. She did not know one of her friends who would turn down a gift like this. She still had her suspicions, and she could not lose focus on what the real picture was for her and Kenyuna.

Karen was feeling uncomfortable with the gifts. They just kept coming. He never came empty-handed; each time he came with stacks of clothes and shoes, and he continued to leave her money in her box. Karen's beliefs were getting the best of her. She knew that what goes around comes around. Karen needed to talk with Rich about what he was doing. It was not working. He was spending too much time with her and not enough time at home with his wife. She could see he was not spending enough time at home. She knew now that something was wrong. He was married, and that was the fact of the matter. She knew she would not be the scapegoat for whatever was wrong with his marriage. She was not the one who was going to fix it; she was not in love with him. It never dawned on her how he felt about her or if he was in love with her. She just said this or that, and he did it sometimes voluntarily without her asking; she was calling her own shots. She was not married. If he wanted out of a bad marriage, then he would have to figure it out on his own. She had to do what was best for her own soul and her self-esteem. She had always prided herself on not being a follower. This situation was not going to define her character and morals now. She waited patiently for Rich to call. She was ready to do battle with her enemy now.

"Hey, we need to talk soon."

"What's wrong?" replied Rich.

"Everything," she told him, "can we talk about it later?"

"Okay, see you later."

She sat at her desk thinking over the last several months of dealing with him, and her conclusion was that it just was not worth it. The few times they were intimate, it just did not do anything for her. She lay there as her mind raced. She asked herself if she had lost her mind. It was the end of it with him. Things just did not get any better. It was why she never bothered with married men anyway; they were too much trouble. She was preparing dinner when the phone rang, much to her surprise. The voice on the other end was not one that she recognized or wanted to ever hear.

"Hello."

"Is this Karen?"

"Yes."

"This is Mrs. Rich. I want to know what is going on with you and my husband."

"Nothing is going on with me and your husband. I suggest you talk with your husband, and please do not call my home again."

Whatever he had done before to keep his wife off his back was not working anymore. It had come crashing down. She was calling to confirm her suspicions. The only thing Karen could hear in the distance was the dial tone of the phone that she had not hung up.

She knew then that this friendship, relationship, or whatever it was, was over. No more contact with Rich; it ended that day.

"What's wrong?"

He stood in her kitchen while she did the dishes over the sink. She turned to face him so that he would get a clear understanding of what she was about to say.

"Rich, this is not working out for the both of us. Today, your wife called my home. She wanted to know what was going on with us. We will no longer have any contact with each other, so please stop calling. And please do not come by my home anymore after today."

Karen noticed he just stood there with a blank expression on his face. He looked directly into her face. She did not know what he would do or what he was going to say. He turned and walked closer to her.

"Karen, you don't mean that. I love you."

"Rich," she said, "you are a married man. You cannot love me. You are married. You knew that, and so did I. Today, I ask that you leave me alone and go home and work on your marriage."

Rich left her apartment with a defeated look on his face. He did not respond to her requests. She had this gut feeling that he was not gone for good. He would not go away that easily. Her instincts were always right, and she appreciated them. He called her daily and continued to leave her gifts. He would sit around her apartment and ring her doorbell, which she refused to answer. She often threatened to call the police or his wife on him. She was determined she had enough of this married man and any other after him; they could keep moving. Her neighbors let her know her friend was at her apartment building, sitting in his car, waiting for her for hours. He rang her doorbell, but they knew she was not home. She hoped he worked through his marriage even through the bad, the ugly, and these hard times. She had seen marriages that worked out and others that did not. She did not want to be a part of either one. She never wanted another woman to call her home looking for her husband. She knew the signs and what it felt like to be on both sides of the fence, watching your marriage fall apart because of the actions of another woman. She knew what it was like to have a husband who had gone astray or lost his way from home. She hoped things would work out for Rich and his wife so that they could mend their broken fence and get back together. Rick was not receiving the message at all. He just kept doing things that were getting under Karen's skin. She knew she would have to do something about it soon. He left notes on her door day and night after she stopped answering his calls. He left several messages at all times of the day or night. He used unlisted numbers to call her that did not show on the caller ID, which she never answered anyway. He would come by and ring her doorbell; he drove from his neighborhood to her neighborhood just to do that.

Rick had those kinds of work hours. He owned his business and had staff that worked for him, so he could leave work at any time. He sat on her doorstep, ringing her doorbell. She told Rick that if he did not leave her alone, she would call the police. She was yelling at him that it was over and to leave her alone. She thought that might have worked. When she looked out the window to check, he was getting into his car to leave. She thought she would have some peace, but it did not last long. Within a few days, he was back ringing the doorbell again.

She tried some nights to just block out the doorbell and the calling of her name in the night. Some nights, the doorbell rang for a short time; some nights it rang with her name being called. She thought this had to stop but did not know how she was going to get him to move on. She had made up her mind that she was moving on without him. She started looking out her window before she left her apartment because she did not know when he would show up. She had to be a little creative, so she started parking her car around the block. She would stand there and look to see if Rick's car was in the area. She then changed her house phone number for the first time since she had moved to the city. She never knew it would get to this point; she was at her wit's end with him. He had caused her to declare war on him. The situation was getting out of hand; she was not going to let this guy mess up her life. She had come too far and worked hard to be where she was now compared to where she had started from.

She was especially protective of Kenyuna and concerned for her safety, even though she was hardly home most of the time. Karen thought, What if Rick thought Kenyuna was her coming home late at night? She would never forgive herself if something happened to her darling daughter. She was as tall as Karen at night; he would not be able to tell if it was her or Kenyuna. Accidents happen to innocent people all the time in a relationship that has gone bad. Karen felt a chill go all over her body as she thought of all the wrong things that could go so badly. The thoughts made her even more determined that Rick would get the message one way or another; it could be the easy way or the hard way. She would let him know for the last time that if he did not leave her alone, she would take all action necessary to protect herself, her home, and her child.

Karen had a flashback to some years ago when this guy she was dating wanted to control her every movement. She was not going back down that road ever again. Her faith had always been the mover in her life; it moved at the right time.

Just when she was at her wit's end, along came a butterfly. He was short, stocky, and somewhat handsome. She met him a few years ago while Kenyuna was still in high school. He was her math teacher and had just gone through a divorce himself. He and Kenyuna had become close; she looked up to him as a father figure, and she had talked to him about her mother. Karen remembered Kenyuna telling her about Mr. Ed, but at the time she was preoccupied. Kenyuna said she told Mr. Ed that her mother was pretty, nice, and single.

"Maybe we should meet each other," he said.

She said she would tell her mother, and she did just that.

"Mom, he really wants to meet you."

"Who?" Karen responded.

"Mr. Ed," replied Kenyuna.

Karen told Kenyuna that she would come to the school on her day off the next week. She would meet Mr. Ed. She only did it because it was important to Kenyuna at the time. She had not been to Kenyuna's school in a while. This would be the opportunity to check on her and talk with her other teachers. Karen sat at her desk with all the things she needed to do for the day as she looked around with nothing pressing to do. She gathered her purse and jacket to head out in the cool of the day as she headed toward Kenyuna's school. The parking lot was full of cars as she drove around looking for an open parking space.

She noticed that someone was leaving a parking space that was a lot closer to the school building. The shoes she was wearing were not for a lot of walking, but they sure did look good on her feet. She walked toward the office to inquire what class Kenyuna was in at this hour. She looked toward the stairs that led to the second floor. Her feet shouted in her head, "Don't do it! Take the elevator."

Karen stood in the doorway of the class for a few minutes until one of the students noticed her standing there. A student shouted to the teacher that someone was standing at the door. The class was loud as the students talked with each other. Karen could see Kenyuna now.

"Hello, can I help you?" A voice called out from behind one of the art stands. Karen did not see the little, petite woman until she stepped from behind the stand and walked towards her.

"Hi, I'm Kenyuna's mother. I just came to check on her to see how she was doing."

"Hi, Mom. What are you doing here?"

"I just came to say hello and see if you want a ride home."

"No, I have baseball practice today. I will get the late bus. Let's go see Mr. Ed. I'll show you where his classroom is."

Karen just smiled as she walked with Kenyuna down the long hallway, as her feet kept talking loudly to her in her ear with every step.

She still had to talk with Kenyuna's counselor today. She thought that if her feet didn't cooperate, she might have to wait another day to see the counselor.

The door was open. He sat at his desk, looking over papers when he heard his name called.

"Mr. Ed, this is my mom, Ms. Karen."

"Nice to meet you," he said as he held his hand out toward her to shake her.

"Nice to finally meet you. I have heard so much about you. You have made a great impression on my daughter; she speaks highly of you often."

"Well, that is nice to know. Thank you for coming."

"I will not hold you up from your work. Have a good evening."

They were walking down the hall towards the counselor's office when Kenyuna said, "See, mom, I told you he was nice and handsome."

She had never seen a desk that looked like that. She knew this would be a very short visit. His desk had stacks of papers everywhere; she could not even imagine that he could find anything. She thought some people were more organized with a messy desk than those with a clean one.

Karen gave her daughter a huge hug and told her she would see her at home later. Kenyuna ran off to her locker to get ready for her baseball practice and to catch up with her friends. Her day was pretty productive as she pushed her way out of the school's front doors, and headed toward her car. She could not wait to get to the car so she could pull these damn shoes off. She put a little pep in her step. She loved a nice-looking pair of shoes. She was just getting too old to deal with her feet hurting at the end of the day from wearing them. This was one of those days that would make her choose comfort over cuteness. The house was dark and quiet. She would soak in a bubble bath with a glass of wine and go to bed early. She had enough excitement today to last her the rest of the week.

She hoped that Rick would just leave her alone just for tonight. It was an easy, fast meal for dinner tonight—something she could put together quickly that would still taste good. She didn't care what the calorie count was going to be tonight; she was not in the mood for anything.

She did not hear Kenyuna come in at all or the alarm clock go off. She rolled over to see the bright letters reading 7:30. She loved the fact that she did not have to get up and go out so early; it was one thing she loved about working part-time. It didn't pay a hell of a lot of money, but it did give her the flexible schedule she needed, and she was thankful for that. She learned to live within her financial budget, even though she still missed the extra cash that Rick gave her from time to time. Karen told herself that the price was just too high for her to continue with the relationship and that she would be done with school in a few semesters. She had to work really hard and complete them in two semesters for sure. The jewelry, clothes, and cash had all come to an end, and she knew it would all be a thing of the past soon. She sure did not know what was in that chocolate box until it was opened. He was determined to have a relationship with her, and the more she told him no, the more he persisted. She took a hard look at what this man was willing to offer her. She asked herself, "Who could resist the opportunity to be given anything they wanted: cash, gifts, dining, and free car repairs?"

She just could not swallow her pride or her spiritual beliefs to be the other woman. She longed for the day that a man would come into her life to do the things that Rich did to be a couple who truly loved each other and wanted to be with each other. Rich was not him.

The quiet did not last for long. He started over with the calls and added a little something to them. He started leaving notes on her car late at night, even when the dogs were trying to sleep. It did not take her off her game; she had been exposed enough in this life to think ahead. She did not even read the cards anymore; she just tore them up, stuck them in her bag, or threw them in the trash, and got where she was going. Rich had long stopped leaving financial gifts. I guess the song is true to its words: "nothing from nothing leaves nothing."

She was awakened by the doorbell, and she rolled over to see the clock. It was 6:00 a.m. She rolled out of bed, thinking it might be an emergency. She did not put on her robe. She hit the light and walked toward the door, calling out. She could see from the upper stairs the door that led to her apartment on the second floor. She felt safe in the second-floor duplex. You could not get in unless you were let in. Then you still had to come up several stairs to enter her apartment. She moved closer to the edge of the stairs to see if she could see someone standing at the door. She turned off the light to see better. She couldn't see anything.

"Who is it?" She yelled again, hoping to get a response without waking Kenyuna with her shouting.

Still, no answer came in return, and she thought that someone had the apartment by mistake. She lived a couple of blocks away from several nightclubs that stayed open until two or three in the morning. It could have been some drunken person who thought they were somewhere they were not. Karen resolved the issue in her mind and headed back inside her apartment toward her bedroom when the doorbell rang again.

"Okay, that's it. What the hell is going on?"

She told herself as she yelled once again downstairs at the door. Still, she did not get an answer. She went back to her bedroom to get her robe and put on some shoes. She got her keys. She checked if she could see anyone before opening the door. She looked out the door with the light off to see if she could see a shadow or anyone around, but she could not see anyone. She slowly unlocked the door and cracked it just enough to look out. She did not see a single person outside among all the many cars that were parked in front of the apartment building. But just as she was about to head back inside, she saw a bunch of flowers and a card sitting in the corner behind the door. She picked them up and headed back upstairs. She dropped them on the dining room table as she headed toward her bedroom. She knew who they were from. There was no need to take any more time out of her night to think about this issue. She had to be up too early to be bothered with Rich. She would deal with another episode tomorrow. She decided it was time to invite Mr. Ed over to keep her company, just in case Rich decided to do something stupid. Rich's behavior was not normal; it was making her feel uneasy. She did not want to take any chances on what he might or might not do. He continued to put notes and flowers on her car and at her door. He called, but not as often, which made her wonder what he was up to. Occasionally, when he did catch her at home, it would be by accident. She spoke with him very briefly and clearly. She had enough; she wanted him to know she would not tolerate his behavior any longer. She had to let him know what they had was over. It would never be again. It would take a few more months before he finally got the message, but the picture became very clear. She thought about an old saying she read somewhere: "Time will heal all wounds if you allow it to." He was becoming a fading memory in her mind. She could hardly remember what had brought her to this point in her life; she had to once again become the villain, or the big B - - - - -.

She settled into her single life once again and enjoyed the freedom of not having anyone special in her life. Freedom at last. She spoke the words in her mind as she drove home alone. The radio played in the distance. A woman's work was never done. She still had to stop by the store to get items for dinner. She needed to look over her bank account before she bounced checks. There was no more extra cash coming from Rich; that was gone now. She needed to start counting her own dollars; she needed to balance it all out herself. She knew she had to support herself for now. She had become a woman who was sure of herself and had to stand on her own two feet. She felt the change from when she was in her twenties and didn't know what she was doing. Now she was a mature, intelligent, educated, and well-rounded adult woman. Things just did not hang her up in this life that she thought she needed; they were gone.

It was not long before another guy caught her attention and interest. This time it would be different than before. She knew that. She knew she had the skills and knowledge to know when to get out and let go. She was now able to do what she wanted to do within any relationship or situation. Alone once again, it did not seem to bother her at all. She had gotten used to making her own decisions and arranging her life, which connected her with Kenyuna. It looked pretty good to her. Her own apartment was fully furnished and well-coordinated; her car was paid for; and she had a bachelor's degree under her belt. She had to keep moving forward and could not look back now at the things that she had lost or missed along the way. She still had the most precious thing that a woman could have, which was her beautiful daughter by her side. She was determined to spare Kenyuna as much heartache in her life as she could, especially less than she had. The bond they shared as mother and daughter was that they each knew what role they played and what parts to participate in to get the best they could from each other. God had mercy on her; she got a pretty good child. She knew Karen loved her and that she was her mother. Karen did not have to beat her to get that point across to her.

Karen was feeling good when something just fell into her lap. She ran into Tracy, who she had worked with at a summer job in the city. They got along pretty well, and as they were talking, she said, "We have a position open. Why don't you come and apply and tell them that I referred you?"

"I applied some months ago," Karen said.

"Even better," she said, "call the receptionist and tell her to pull your application and give it to the director. We will call you for an interview."

"Thanks. How much does the job pay?"

"Well, it would depend on your degree."

"I have a degree in liberal arts studies."

"With the degree you have, you should start out making the top rate on the pay scale."

Karen's hair stood on the back of her neck, and her insides jumped with joy. Karen was already working for the Census Bureau at the time, and that job would be done within a few months; she was already looking for another job at the time. She knew that faith was on her side and that she was heading in the right direction.

Karen used the college computer to create a resume and fine-tuned her wardrobe with pieces she already had from the clothes that Rich had given her. She purchased a few more shoes. She needed the basic colors that would go with all the outfits she wore. She was ready to get down to business. She could live pretty well off a good salary and could afford to put a little aside for a house in the future.

Karen made that call and sent her resume as requested. A few weeks had gone by when she received a message for an interview. She was nervous as she walked into the building. She gathered herself and took a look in the mirror at her hair and makeup. She walked into an office where a Hispanic lady looked up from her desk.

"Can I help you?" she asked.

"I have an interview at 11:00 a.m.," Karen replied.

"Have a seat, and someone will be with you shortly."

Karen's stomach was in knots; she could feel her body beginning to sweat inside her clothes. She told herself to take a deep breath and relax. She could do this. It had always been hard for her to walk into a room with people she did not know and not have a clue what questions would be asked of her. Karen knew she could do her best and come up with the right answers to any question asked of her. She had good old common sense, spiritual sense, and street smarts; she knew she could pull this interview off. She was called into a large classroom with a table and eight chairs, but only four were occupied.

A large lady sat in one chair, a Hispanic lady in another, a Caucasian lady in another, and Tracy was in the fourth chair. Karen's nervousness settled down when she saw Tracy. It was a relief to see someone she could relate to, even for a short time. Karen heard a voice in the direction of the door tell her to come in and have a seat. She moved toward the vacant chair. She placed her resume in the folder on the table and put her purse on the table, pulling herself closer to the table.

One after the other, they asked questions from the document in front of them, quietly writing down her answers. What seemed like forever only took about an hour. Karen heard one of the ladies say, "Thank you for coming in; we appreciate you interviewing with us. You will get a letter from our office regarding employment with us soon."

"I appreciate you taking the time out of your busy day to interview me. Have a nice day."

She walked out feeling like she had gotten the job; she had felt this way before and not gotten the job, so she would just pray and wait. She told herself that even if she did not get the job, she still had an income from her job at Census Bureau that would hold her over until something else came along. She still had about three to six months of work to do with that job that paid her every week. Karen waited and waited for the call. It had been about two weeks, but there was no letter in the mail. She told herself that no news was good news and to just be patient. She knew that when you want to work for the federal government, they do all kinds of background checks—criminal records, child abuse records, and all the states that you have ever lived in. She knew that she had lived in other states than this one. She looked at it that way and moved on with what she needed to do.

BUTTERFLY NINE: KEEP IT MOVING

Karen made a list of things that she could not put off any longer and had to get done. One of those was to make an appointment to visit Kenyuna's teachers for a conference to see how she was doing in school. She would be graduating in the fall. Karen wanted to make sure she had all her credits to graduate. Karen knew what it was like to go to school for twelve years and find out later on her education journey that she needed half a credit to get her diploma. Karen was not about to let that stupid mistake happen to Kenyuna. She took one whole day off work to make sure. She wanted to talk with each teacher and the school counselor. She did not want to leave any stone unturned. She walked down each hall, seeing each teacher. She even saw Kenyuna in her math class.

Karen walked into a classroom, where a black male teacher met her at the door. Karen met some of Kenyuna's school friends as the class was coming to an end. She was glad she had taken the time out of her day to visit. Karen was on edge about Mr. Ed. She knew how predators warm up to a little girl and then take advantage of her. Her child was not going to be in those statistics. She was definitely going to keep an eye on Mr. Ed. She came back to her senses when the front door of the car swung open. Kenyuna was talking even before she could get into the car.

"Mom, how was your day? Why did you not tell me you were coming to school?"

"Child, you don't need to know where I am going to be. I just pop up when you least expect me to."

"Well, what do you think about Mr. Ed?"

"He seems like a nice man. He is handsome, just like you said. I had a great day. You have some nice teachers, and they said that you are doing well in their class. That's all that matters to me."

The car was quiet as the music played on the radio. Kenyuna looked over some papers and turned the radio to a station that suited her taste. The apartment was dark when they entered the door; there were several stairs to climb.

Karen heard the dogs barking outside. She was happy that she did not have any studying to do—no more books to read and no more late-night papers to write. For a long time, it seemed she had not come home to do what she wanted to do. Tonight she would watch a movie, go to bed early, and not feel guilty if she did not cook a thing. That's the life. Kenyuna was now old enough to feed herself, and she could give her a few dollars to let her decide what she wanted to eat. Karen made sure there was always something worth eating in the icebox in the kitchen. Her cooking habit had changed over the years from cooking for a family of ten to twelve at her parent's house, then for three when she was married, and now for her and Kenyuna only. It felt kind of weird, but it felt great to her as she lay in the tub with a candle and a glass of chilled red wine. The phone rang, and she just let the answering machine get it as she slipped further into the tub, running more warm water, which made more bubbles. She walked out of the bathroom and down the hall to Kenyuna's room to check on her before she headed to bed. She could hear her television playing and thought of the thousands of times she had told her not to go to sleep with that television left on. She knew that was just her talking to herself. Kenyuna was asleep. She moved to turn the TV off and quietly left the room. Her bed was calling her too. She was answering it in her mind as she flipped the channel to the news, pulled the covers back on the bed, and snuggled in. Adjusting the pillows, she put the remote in bed with her to set the sleep timer on the TV so it would go off whether she fell asleep or not, which would most likely be the case tonight. She looked over at her answering machine and saw that she had several messages. She was not going to return anyone's phone call tonight. She would get back to whoever tomorrow at the earliest; she hoped that none of the messages were emergencies. She said her prayer and turned off the light as the news watched her go off to sleep land. Awakened by the phone, she rolled over and answered.

"Hello."

"Girl, are you still asleep?"

"Yes, what's up?"

"I'll call you back."

"Okay, bye."

Karen felt for the phone to hang up with her eyes still closed. She rolled over, pulled the covers up around her head, and went back to sleep. She felt Kenyuna climb into bed with her, and they lay sleeping until midmorning. Karen left Kenyuna in her bed as she headed to the kitchen to see what would be good for breakfast. She was glad it was a Saturday. Usually, it was a big breakfast day to eat and hang around the house. She always thought running to the grocery store on Saturday took up most of her day. She hated going grocery shopping on Saturdays; there were too many people and too much traffic. She made it a point to have everything she needed in the kitchen before the weekend. Her schedule permitted her to go to the grocery store anytime during the week to pick up whatever she needed. She looked to see what they had: fried potatoes, sausage, eggs, biscuits, and preserver. The house was too quiet when she turned on the radio. She kept it low so that it would not wake Kenyuna. Her days were as long as her days. She let the dog in for company even though she knew the dog would lie under the small table just looking and waiting for something to fall to the floor. Karen thought dogs had the easiest job in the world. They ate for free and had free rooms. What a great life! Wiping her eyes, Kenyuna looked into the kitchen.

"Hey, Mom."

"Good morning, Kenyuna," she replied.

Kenyuna headed toward the bathroom. Karen continued with breakfast, thankful that she may not be rich, but she was well on her way to being wealthy someday. She could feel it. She knew that one day it would be. They enjoyed the home-cooked breakfast. She was thankful to her mother for teaching her how to cook even when she did not want to learn. She bit into the Pillsbury biscuit that was not burned. The dough was just right, and with that buttery taste and that preserver on it, she could just get up and do a dance; it tasted that good. Kenyuna seemed to enjoy her breakfast as well. Karen's belly was full, and bills were paid. She headed back to her bedroom, closed her door, and lay in bed, falling back to sleep. Ring! She heard it in her sleep, thinking it was just a dream until the sound became more real to her ears and she realized it was the phone ringing. Today was a rest day for her. She had nothing much planned for the day except to lay around and take it easy. She fixed herself another cup of coffee and sat at the kitchen table, taking in the quietness of the morning. It was nice not to have to do anything this morning. She had no real downtime like this for a long time, it seemed. Between school, working, and running a household, there was just not enough time for Karen to appreciate what she should be grateful for in her life at this time. She looked around at the apartment filled with some new and used furniture she had purchased over the years, and a smile came over her face. She realized she had done what she thought she could not do some years ago. Kenyuna had graduated from high school and a two-year college. It was time to move on from here. She felt she was unstoppable. Her time had finally come. No more drama in her life felt pretty good. She felt so free at the moment, sitting there sipping on her warm cup of coffee. Free at last, free at last, thank almighty God, I feel free at last. She sat for a few hours in the quiet, all alone with her thoughts.

The weekend always seems to go faster than the weekday. It did not bother Karen that it was Monday morning already. She was refreshed and ready for another week. The weekend's rest had done her good. She would do this for herself as often as she could. This would be a retreat for her even if she did not go on a luxury trip. Staying at home would be one of the best things for her mental health. She could go anywhere she wanted to. She knew it would be, and so it was. Things were looking even better now that she had a full-time job; the bills were getting paid with some extra funds left over. She loved her apartment, but things were getting a little uncomfortable in the city for her. She knew that she would not find another deal like this anywhere else close to the downtown area: lots of car traffic, sirens, and a lot of foot traffic, but the location was great. The area was getting a lot of unknown visitors walking around all hours of the night as it was changing. Several clubs had opened since she moved to the area. She could hear more and more loud noises at night than she wanted to. Some nights, she would be awakened by intoxicated people outside her apartment arguing back and forth with each other. It could last for an hour. She would just get out of bed and look out the window, seeing two drunk people disturbing her sleep. Once or twice, she had to call the police because the discussion would be so intense that she did not want anyone to get hurt.

This night was no different, and she had a long day. She just wanted to get in bed and have a good night's sleep. Just as she was getting into a deep sleep, she started hearing cussing, threatening, and yelling. Not tonight, she told herself. Looking down out the window, there were two males who were drunk and talking about who would be driving the car, which neither one was in any condition to drive. She called 911 and reported the disturbance outside of her apartment. A few minutes later, she could hear the siren outside her apartment.

"Thank God," she said and headed back to bed.

She heard the sirens stop on the side of her apartment and the officers talking with the drunken idiots outside.

Shortly after, the noise was gone, but she could not get back to sleep. She decided then that it was time to move to a new place. Tomorrow, she would start looking for a house in a good neighborhood without all this drama going on. This area had just gotten too dangerous for her to be coming in at night, sometimes late into the night. Kenyuna was getting too acquainted with the young men and boys hanging out in the area. Karen knew some of them; she did not want to know the others, and she knew what kinds of illegal activities they were into as well. They were out most of the night and all hours of the day, which was not a good sign that they were doing anything productive. She did not want Kenyuna to get involved in that lifestyle, for sure. She considered herself book smart, but she had full knowledge of how the criminal elements of the streets worked as well.

Karen pulled her credit report, not knowing what it would show after the divorce and the bankruptcy she had filed several years ago. She was willing to repair any damage to correct it. She had no choice if she was going to move out of that area. She was determined to do just that.

She found her credit report was not as bad as she had thought. It was in pretty good shape. It didn't have that car she had co-signed for Kenyuna about two years ago with a judgment attached of a few thousand dollars; it wasn't even there. She figured she would work out a payment arrangement with the collector to pay it off. She had a few credit cards with a few thousand on each of them that she could pay off before she found the house. She said to herself that it could be worked out with discipline, self-control, and a budget for her spending. Her new job paid her a pretty good salary. Kenyuna was buying her own clothing and whatever personal items she needed while still working part-time and going to Code Billing College.

Karen knew that it was time to get moving. If she was going to move at all, the time was now. In her spare time, she would go to different neighborhoods she had driven to before, wishing she could live there someday. She had already been to an area she had liked over the years and often shopped at in the city. She never wanted to live so far from her work; she only wanted to live and drive fifteen to twenty minutes to any job. The location would make or break her.

She knew this would play a major role in where she would land for the next phase of her life. Months turned into a year. Karen had looked for at least a few houses a week when her schedule permitted. Some houses were too expensive for her price range or not in the right area. She even tried the realtor route, but they wanted to put her where they thought was the right place for them. She soon dropped the realtors and went at it on her own. She knew that God knew her heart and that the right house was out there for her. She would be her own key to success; she would let it have its way by leaning on her faith. Early on a Saturday morning, she wanted to go to an area where she often went shopping, a few miles away from her apartment. It was a straight shot to the area.

She liked this part of the city because it had all the exits that could take you to any part of the city via the freeway, or you could just drive the straight street from the north and back to the south. She was done with her shopping and decided to check out some of the neighborhoods in the area. She could feel the excitement in her chest when she saw the first subdivision. The sidewalks were well taken care of, the yards were manicured, and the homes were beautiful. She drove for hours just looking and taking down the numbers from for-sale signs in the yards. Plenty of the houses on the market interested her. She could not wait to get her eyes inside to see what was available for her. She also could not wait to tell Kenyuna about the good news and show her all the houses she had found for sale. She had all the groceries inside and was putting them away when she heard Kenyuna coming inside the door. She could hardly keep herself from jumping up from the couch.

"Kenyuna, come," she yelled, "I have something to show you."

She shared the good news with Kenyuna and discussed that it was time to move. Kenyuna was all in, and that was all Karen needed to hear from her. Kenyuna felt that it was time for a change as well. They had become very close over the years. They knew they were all they had. They had come through some hard times over the years, but things were finally looking up for both of them.

Karen made some phone calls the next day, right after church. She wanted to see what houses were open for her and Kenyuna to check out. She made an appointment to see a few houses every day that same week. She knew that whatever house she picked would have to be equal to or more than what she had been living in over the last few years. It had to have the amenities of three bedrooms, two full bathrooms, and central air conditioning. She knew she would not be able to live without those amenities. Another thing she could not live without was a place where she could get quiet. She needed a spare room in which she could work on her little project or do nothing. She would not settle for not having three bedrooms in the house. Maybe someday she would be a grannie, and she would be glad to give that room up for that for sure. That was not in Kenyuna's plans. She was not considering having children now or in the future. She had often told Karen that she did not want any children. Karen did not push the issue with her, nor did she try to change her mind. Karen would let Kenyuna grow and make her own grown-up decisions on how she wanted her life to be. Karen had decided years before not to be a parent who wanted to live out her life by dictating the way her child should live hers. Karen moved on with her life, and Kenyuna could come if she wanted to. Either way was fine with her. She was moving on regardless.

House appointments kept her busy, and she was having a hard time finding the house she was looking for. It was getting to be long days and nights looking at houses—several houses a week and several over the weekend. Karen decided she would give house hunting a break and give herself a weekend break to relax and do nothing. She could not believe she had slept until noon before she rolled over and saw the clock on the nightstand.

The apartment was quiet; she assumed that Kenyuna had left for the day. She threw the covers off and rolled out of bed, heading toward the bathroom. Kenyuna's door was closed when she peeked in to find her still asleep in bed. Karen closed the door and smiled to herself, thinking Kenyuna must have needed the rest as much as she did. Coffee was what she needed now. She turned toward the kitchen to turn on the coffee pot. She took her cup of coffee and moved back toward her bedroom. She did not even want to cook breakfast; she just wanted to get back in bed and let the day move on. Karen turned on the television while she sat on the edge of the bed, sipping her coffee. She went back to sleep until it was dark outside before she woke up.

Kenyuna had left for work. She knew how to be very quiet when Karen was sleeping. Karen did not even hear her leave the apartment. Karen moved from room to room, turning on the lights. Her stomach was speaking to her with the roaring sounds of hunger. Chinese food sounded really good. She had not taken anything out of the refrigerator to cook. She called to place her order. She told them she would be there to get her order within fifteen to twenty minutes. She put her house slippers on in her PJs, brushed her hair back, and grabbed her keys, heading out the door. She loved Chinese food. It never dissatisfied her. She had this Chinese restaurant not far from her apartment that she liked a lot, and they knew her as a customer.

Satisfied and full, she placed the rest of the Chinese food in the refrigerator just in case Kenyuna would come home hungry too, but if not, she would surely eat the rest later. It was showtime. She took a glass of wine and looked in the closet for what she would be wearing to work tomorrow. She could hear the news on the television in the background but paid very little attention to it. She put a CD in the player and headed into the bathroom, which would be her stop for a while. She hated Mondays. She did not look forward to them at all. She had always wondered who in the hell decided that people should work five days with only two days off. That was just not enough days off and too many days working to make a living. Karen lay in bed on Mondays until the last minute before she knew it was the last time she could hit the alarm clock again. She knew she would have lots of work to do on Monday and that everybody and their moms would be looking for her, wanting her attention, and she hated the demands.

This day could not be over for me soon enough, she thought as she locked the door to the apartment. The days would not be lost in total. She had three house appointments after work, a schedule she kept for the long summer days to be out of this apartment. It was summer. The days were long and beautiful, and the air smelled a lot different than in the winter months. She could see many houses and still make it home before it got too dark. So far, none of the houses fit her list of wants. She was done, so she headed home. Kenyuna was on the phone when Karen got home.

"Hello!" Karen yelled, but she did not stop her conversation on the phone.

BUTTERFLY TEN: HE CAME UNFAITHFUL

He was just too good to be true. Karen felt it deep down inside; she knew what that felt like. This time around, she was not going to ignore it. She had decided that she was not going to jump into another relationship without checking out the person's intentions and motives. Kenyuna had spoken so highly of Mr. Stocky. She finally decided to call the number he had given her. To her, he was just her math teacher during her last year of high school. Karen had met him. They spoke with each other over the school year. He seemed to be a pleasant man, but she never gave him any thought. She was busy wrapping up and getting out of a relationship that had taken its toll on her for almost a year. The phone rang, and she got a little nervous. This was out of her comfort zone. She remembered her father telling her, "If a man wanted you, he would call you." She knew she should have lived by his words. But she told herself that times had changed and it was not a big deal if a woman called a man in today's time. Who cares about who called first anyway?

His voice was deep and professional; the conversation was an easy one to have as the conversation flowed with ease. They made plans to meet for dinner in a few days. He said he would call her back with the date and time by the weekend. She was happy that his conversation stimulated her mind. He had a very easy and smooth voice. She did not feel a connection with Mr. Stocky, nor did he leave her with any feelings. Whether he called her back or not, it would not bother her either way.

The week moved by pretty quickly. It was Friday, and Karen was glad she had planned just to relax and maybe catch up on some movies she had not seen because of her busy schedule. She grabbed a bottle of wine on her way home from the liquor store. It would be an evening on the couch with me, myself, and I. Kenyuna would be out with her friends for the evening; she might not see her until later that evening or night.

She put her bags on the table and headed toward the bedroom to get out of her clothes. She could not wait to shower and slip on her pajamas with her house shoes. She started to remove her makeup, wanting to forget about the hustles and bustles of the day. She was not expecting company tonight. She did not want to be bothered when the phone rang. It was Mr. Stocky on the other end.

"Hello, do you have any plans for the evening?"

"No, I don't."

"Great! Can I come over to see you later tonight if that's alright with you?"

Karen felt a strange feeling in her stomach and wondered what this man's motive was; she was not sure about him yet.

"I've just gotten in from work, and I'll need a little time to get myself together. Can you call me back in a few hours?"

Karen could not get an understanding of Mr. Stocky; she knew that there was something just not right about this guy. She knew that gut feeling and what it felt like—she just could. He was just too smooth for his own good. She would just go along until she found out his angle. A few hours had passed when the phone rang again. It was him saying that he was on his way. Karen's reply was okay. She sat on the couch with thoughts going around in her head as she tried to settle them down with another glass of wine.

She had not known Mr. Stocky for that long, maybe a few months, but tonight the physical chemistry was mutual between the both of them. Maybe tonight she would put her uneasy feeling aside and let the night move in a direction that would benefit her natural side. The conversation was nothing deep, and the movie that was playing was not keeping his attention. She felt his hand rubbing her arm. She lay next to him with his arm around her. She tried to stay focused on the movie, but his hand was just so soft that it took all her attention away from the movie. She closed her eyes and went with the flow. He began to rub her hair and touch her face gently. She rolled to face him. His head leaned down and began kissing her. Then she stood up and grabbed him by the hand. They both headed toward her bedroom until about midnight.

Mr. Stocky got out of bed and began to get dressed to leave. Karen did not know what to say or think. She just did not want Kenyuna to come home to find her ex-math teacher in bed with her mother. Karen felt that Mr. Stocky did not want that either; there were few words spoken as he continued to dress in the half-dark room. She felt the feeling was mutual and that children should not know about their parents' sexual affairs. Karen knew Mr. Stocky had a daughter a few years older than Kenyuna. From the conversations they shared, he seemed to love her almost as much as Karen loved Kenyuuna. Karen slipped on her robe and followed him to the door. He turned to kiss her on the cheek.

"Good morning," she said.

"Good morning. I'll call you later."

She headed back to bed, where she fell into a deep sleep. She heard Kenyuna coming up the stairs from the back door entranceway. What timing or luck, she thought. It had only been about fifteen minutes since Mr. Stocky left through the front door. Karen lay quietly and dozed off to sleep once she heard Kenyuna close her bedroom door. She was almost waiting for her to come in and say that she had seen Mr. Stocky outside or something, but she did not. Karen was glad they had not crossed paths that night.

A few more weeks passed. Karen just could not get that uneasy feeling to go away about Mr. Stocky. He had not invited her over to his house on the few dinner dates they did have, and when she inquired about an invite, he just beat around the bush, giving excuses. That made her even more suspicious and determined to find out what kind of game he was trying to play with her.

She invited him over for dinner. She was going to get some answers from him one way or another once and for all. She was going to be direct and to the point with him; she had plans and did not need to waste any time with deceitful people. It was 6:00 p.m. when Karen heard the doorbell ring. She ran down the long stairs to greet her guest at the door. There he stood, handsome, wearing a nicely pressed shirt and slacks with creases as sharp as his smile and touch. Karen had prepared one of her favorite dishes; everything was ready, even her. She led the way to the kitchen, handed him a plate, and gently placed the lasagna, corn, and French toast on it. She filled her plate as they both headed toward the dining room, where Mr. Stocky sat across the table from her. She wanted to hear and see his expression in response to the questions she had in store for him tonight. Karen did not know what he had in mind for her tonight, but whatever it was, it was not going to fly tonight. She had to get this uneasy feeling about him off her chest, and tonight was the night. They ate in silence, looking at each other across the table and smiling.

"Dinner is delicious," he said. "Most black women don't cook these days or don't know how to cook."

"Learning to cook was one of her mother's requirements for her daughter," she replied. "Plus, eating out regularly doesn't always work with my budget."

Mr. Stocky laughed, thinking that it was funny.

He doesn't know I'm not joking, she thought.

Her income was not for eating out regularly; she was working on repairing her damaged credit report and purchasing a home soon.

Karen started the conversation by saying, "We need to talk."

They both sat in a large chair, and she sat in his lap.

"Are you married?"

"No, I'm not married now. I was some years ago, but I'm divorced now."

He continued to share that during the marriage, they had two daughters—one of whom still lived with him and was going to college in the city. He shared that he was a pastor, although he was not ministering to any church congregation at the time. Karen could have fallen off his lap, but she kept herself composed as he continued to enlighten her with his plans. He had applied to several churches to be the pastor in other states, but none had replied to him yet. He shared that he was waiting for his daughter to graduate from college within the next few months, after which the school year would be complete and he would retire. This was his plan, and it did match her plans. He was determined to become a pastor and move to whatever church would take him to pastor their congregation; this was his decision. She removed herself from his lap.

"When were you going to tell me all his future plans if I hadn't asked?"

She would be just a puppy hanging on a string, waiting for something to happen that would never happen. She was happy that she had her own plans in place and that he was not included either.

"Well," he said, "my plans are not going to happen right away. I still have the rest of the school year to finish. We can continue dating and enjoying each other's company till then."

Some butterflies look so beautiful that you forget to look closer to see what they are and take in their beauty, but they fly on by. Karen knew Mr. Stocky was one of those butterflies that you just let fly away in the wind. She was not going to put her plans on hold for someone whose plans did not include her. They moved to the sofa. She knew that was the end of the relationship and the nights they would spend together. It was the best for both of them. She had all the answers she needed for herself to make the right decision.

Weeks passed, and they continued with their routine as school was coming to an end. Mr. Stocky called to take her out to the lake to enjoy a warm summer evening. They sat at a picnic table, looking across the shadow of the lake as the sun went down in the distance. It was quiet and peaceful, a calmness she could hear aside from the other people in a short distance enjoying the lake site as well.

Mr. Stocky shared with Karen that he had accepted a pastoral position with a church in Georgia. She was not surprised or excited for him. She had prepared herself for this day, waiting for it to continue. He proceeded to tell her he wanted her to continue to be in his life and that he would come back and would love to see her. Karen told him she would not be waiting around for him, and she wished him well. She knew her facial expression had changed. Her emotion was something she had no control over, but she was surprised at his gall and nerve. They hugged and kissed each other underneath the bright, shining moon now in the distance to their farewell. It was getting late, and the drive was a silent ride back to the apartment. They held hands the whole way. She hoped that she could just make it home without crying and with limited conversation. All had been said, and there was nothing else to be said. When the car door opened, Mr. Stocky grabbed her close to him. They both said goodbye with a long hug. She headed toward her apartment. He could not see her tears. She heard him close the car door and drive off.

She did not look back. She kept walking as Mr. Stocky drove away. She knew she would never hear from him again or see him again. It was well with her soul. While undressing for bed, she thought she was done with all her butterflies. For a while, there was no one she had to call tonight or even expected to see. No more. They had all flown away, and she felt at peace with it. Tomorrow, and from that point on, she had her own plans to work on for what she wanted to do in her new life. She still had her new job, her house hunting was going well, and she had her education. Kenyuna was working toward completing her coding classes, but her ex-husband was nowhere to be found for any child support. She felt she was not in a bad place at all. She got under the warm covers that waited for her. Right before she ended the day, she thanked God for the day and fell fast asleep.

Acknowledgements

To my Family and Friends who has waited so patiently for me to finish this book well it is finished and I hope you have a E-book, hard copy in your hand. I want to say thank you for waiting for me. A special thanks to my love ones who asked often when is the book going to be done. Sometimes the timing my not be right in your life and life just keep getting in the way to keeps you from doing what you want to do. Even at that time life is still their keeping you from moving forward. I made time act right for me now it's time now for me. This is just a new journey I am on that has been one I been on for a little while and it has been worth it. I would not change anything about this journey it was so worth it. Thank to my mother who is not with me in the physical but is always with me in spirit and my heart.

Let me say excuse me for any words not spelled right and/or my grammar that does not sound like what you would write. Thank you anyway if you purchase this book and I hope I can write more stories in the near future that can be enjoyable. I started my next journey of writing my second book and hope it will be on out so much sooner then this one. To those who have a passion of doing something creative, fun, and enjoy do it go for it. It is never to late as long as you have breath in you body to do you. I hope I have made my mother proud and I truly thank her for giving me life may she rest well. You never know what you have until it's gone. Peace and love to all.

Author
Madam CJ. Wells

Don't miss out!

Visit the website below and you can sign up to receive emails whenever Carolyn Wells publishes a new book. There's no charge and no obligation.

https://books2read.com/r/B-A-YORX-PUYHC

BOOKS 2 READ

Connecting independent readers to independent writers.

www.ingramcontent.com/pod-product-compliance
Lightning Source LLC
Chambersburg PA
CBHW060355180626
46817CB00008B/3019